A LADY

IN

SEARCH OF A HUSBAND.

A ROMANCE,

LONDON:

PREFACE.

MANY remarks are unnecessary in presenting this work in a collective shape to the public, as the stamp of their approbation has already been affixed to it.

The scene is laid in the United States, and the characters drawn are those of individuals to be met with every day in respectable American society.

"One touch of nature makes the whole world kin;"

and certain we are that the witty and well-informed female portraitures to be found in this work are more faithfully delineated than the highly coloured sketches of our satirical tourists, our Trollopes and Marryats, and more likely to prove acceptable to the unprejudiced English reader.

The proceedings of the heroine of the story, Miss Kate Marvin, are shrouded in mystery till the last chapter, and the reader is kept in continual wonderment, how such a charming personage can for so long a period remain "a lady in search of a husband." Nor shall we here lift the veil, but, having provided the feast, invite the reader to fall to,—and "may digestion wait on appetite."

London, October. 1847.

A LADY
IN SEARCH OF A HUSBAND.

𝔄 Nobel.

CHAPTER I.

An elegant writer has inquired, "What is woman's life, but a journal of her heart?" to which I will add, what is a journal of her heart, but an account of her search for a husband?

To "get married" seems to be the leading object of her ambition, and to this, every step is considered gradatory. It is the first idea that a girl receives, and, I believe, it is the last which animates the breast of woman—unless, indeed, she gains the summit of her wishes; and then—— but no, we will leave that thought to individual suggestion.

It was a bright summer afternoon. The atmosphere was rife with gladness, and as the sun bathed each nook and glade with its own flooding light, a small party of ladies were seen wending their way to the house of one of their neighbours—situated about half a mile from what was denominated "the village."

As ladies generally require half an hour to exchange the customary salutations and make the usual inquiries, ere they reach subjects of greater interest, we will allow them to pass on before us, while we take a view of the quiet scene.

It is beautiful! or rather, its stillness and harmony dispose us to feel gratification from the appearances of industry, comfort, and thrift.

The village was composed of some half-dozen dwelling-houses, a meeting-house, tavern and store—which in the country mean the receptacle of all " things usually called for"—and a blacksmith's shop. The doctor's and lawyer's offices were yet to be built and filled; inasmuch as the village at the other part of the town had both of these professions, and they considered it their prerogative to watch over the interest of all their neighbours, however distant the location might be.

The house, towards which the ladies were bending their footsteps, was contrary to American custom, situated back from the road. It was surrounded on the south, (or front) and on the west, by an extensive garden of flowers and shrubs. The rear was well stocked with vegetables, and contained the various offices of the household. On the east there was an orchard, well filled with various fruit trees incident to the soil and climate. Eastward, the ground rose in a gentle swell which terminated in a hill at a little distance. On the north, the ascent was more abrupt, and hid the view from sight.

In the back-ground, but screened from view of the house by the hill to the east, there arose a low range of mountains, extending from north to south along the whole horizon. At the west, could be seen the sinuous windings of a beautiful river, graced by its pleasant meadows, and the happy homes of the peaceful and satisfied occupants; and, far in the distance, could be descried the blue and cloud-like waters of an " inland sea."

The doors and windows of the house were all open, and a sound of merriment issued from the apartment where the company were assembled. The next instant a young lady appeared, and as she was passing out of the door, turned to reply to some remark addressed to her from within.

"As you say, ladies," she replied; " I know nothing of the strength of woman's affections. My heart still slumbers in peace and with its own passions—I may love as wildly as any of my sex; but still, I believe, that if I once had loved and doubted, there would be no forgiveness. I will not presume to say that I might not be made a fool of once, but if I were again, I should deserve my fate!" and the speaker bounded off, with a merry laugh leaving her opponents to finish their arguments, or scandal, at their leisure.

Her proud asseverations had been provoked by some gossip of love, jealousy, and deceit; and finding that the numbers, if not their arguments, were more than she wished to encounter, she beat a retreat, and sought the garden.

Catherine Marvin (to introduce the lady more formally to our readers,) was scarce seventeen. She was proud, generous, frank, and kind; but withal, there was a sprinkling of self-will and independence in her composition, not always considered consistent in the gentler sex, by those who look upon them as the mere creatures of obedience. She was mirthful and glad, sad, or serious, like the changing sky of spring-time. Her character remained for time and circumstances to determine. She was but the germ, and cultivation only would decide whether it was to become a thistle or a rose.

In person, she was tall and majestic, rather than fairy-like. Her face was oval, the mouth in repose bespoke warm and gentle passions; but, under excitement, could contract into determination or arch into bitter scorn. Her nose was inexpressive, and seemed placed rather to fulfil the duties of a nose, than indicative of character, Lavater to the contrary notwithstanding. Large dark eyes, full of soul and meaning—tender, merry, or wrathful, as the mood was; with a broad intellectual forehead, dark-brown hair, and a brunette complexion—and now you have the detail of her personal appearance.

Soon after she had passed into the garden, a stranger paused at the gate, and she advanced to learn his errand.

"Miss," without preface, he inquired, "have you seen my son?"

"Your son?" she repeated interrogatively, as she scanned the inquirer, doubting his sanity. But finding nothing to justify the suspicion, a half-merry, half-quizzical look darted from her eyes. The old gentleman noticed it, and replied somewhat tartly,—

"Yes, miss, my son. He left me at the tavern an hour since, to call upon Mr. Marvin, who, I am told, resides here."

"As you are a stranger, sir, pardon me for not having an intuitive knowledge of your son. However, if you will furnish me with a description of his person, I will send a messenger to my father, to inquire if he has seen him."

The old gentleman was now quite wrathy; for fractious persons generally proportion their anger to the superlative degree, in cases where the blunder is their own. This amused Catherine the more, but her mirth was cut short by the approach of the person in question, who courteously saluted her as his father turned abruptly away.

CHAPTER II

"Trifles light as air," weave the net of bliss or misery in human life—especially in the case of a young girl. A look, or word, an irrepressible smile, even though it may be at the most ludicrous, may permanently affect the happiness of her after life; for girls are considered but the beings of dependence, placed upon a circular track, never to be verged from. One false step to the right or left—and they are lost for ever.

I never looked upon a young girl with a sunny eye, an open brow, and a smiling lip, but my head ached to think of the blighted feelings, the repressed aspirations, and destroyed hopes that must attend her future life—unless, happily, education should transform her into an automaton of conventional rules and prescribed duties.

Kate was very particular in inquiring of her father when he returned, who his visitor was; and learned in reply, that he was a young physician who contemplated removing to their village, and that his name was Parker. She gleefully related her encounter with his father, and received a gentle reproof from her mother, while her father declared, that "Kate had not said anything out of the way."

To enter more fully into our biographical detail; Mr. Marvin was a farmer in one of our New England States, more renowned for the intelligence, patriotism, and morality of its inhabitants, than for the fertility of its soil, or its internal improvements. At the time our tale commences, he was somewhat advanced in years, and having formed a later marriage than is usual among farmers, his only child, his pet Kate, was just advancing upon the stage of action.

His wife was all that a husband could wish—that is, if all husbands possessed Mr. Marvin's taste in such matters. She was an excellent housewife, kind, amiable, and considerate; and above all, possessed an exalted opinion of her husband, and loved him with her whole heart. Kate, like all daughters, was considered a wife in prospective—and her father hoped she would make as good a one as her mother had proved.

Happy, even beyond his most sanguine expectation in his domestic relations, if he ever had any regret, it was that he had not married at an earlier period.

In his social position, Mr. Marvin was much esteemed and respected, ever filling the most honourable offices in the gift of his fellow-townsmen. In a pecuniary view, he was wealthy, for although not possessed of many thousands, he was an independent farmer; and independence, in point of fact, is the true criterion of wealth.

In the evening, as Catherine sat upon the piazza in front of the house, either dreaming or thinking, she was aroused by a footstep beside her.

"Good evening, Catherine—Miss Marvin," said a low, manly, but musical voice at her side.

"Ah! good evening—is it you, Legrand? I did not notice your approach;" and she arose to enter the house.

"Nay, stay," said the young man; "I would converse with you a few moments without other company."

Catherine, surprised at the request resumed her seat.

The young man might have been eighteen years of age. His form was slight, but finely developed, giving evidence of much muscular power. His face was not handsome, and at this time, the expression was saddened. His hair was of a very dark-brown, and quite long, clustering around his neck in natural ringlets, and carelessly parted in front, revealing an ample forehead.

His eyes were large and dark. When animated, they seemed black; but usually, as now, there was a deep melancholy expressed in their depths. The colour was not black, neither was it blue or hazel, out perhaps a mixture of all these. In his manners, he was graceful and polite, rather from the intuitive perception of a mind naturally refined and benevolent, than from the conventional polish of society.

There was something of mystery connected with him; and that it had never been penetrated by the good gossips of the vicinity, had invested him with many of the prerogatives which belong to the proud, the aristocratic, the eccentric.

About three years previously, a lady-stranger had arrived in the village, and without any ostensible purpose, had remained there for weeks. Her time was mostly spent in viewing and wandering over the romantic environs of the place. She had no communication with the inhabitants, and even when spoken to, there was a peculiar sententiousness in her answers which prevented any further wish for intercourse.

Her manners were easy and lady-llke. She might have been forty or forty-five years of age, but she was so extremely delicate and fair, that she did not appear much above thirty. She gave no name, and was [only known as the "lady-stranger."

Legrand, then about fifteen, was with her, and apparently was her son. He mingled freely with the youths of the village, and soon became foremost in sport, and most active in harmless mischief; but if casually questioned of his mother, there would instantly steal over his face a deep shadow of thought and pain. The reluctance which his replies evinced, soon caused the villagers to restrain their curiosity; or, perhaps, for a better cause they ceased to annoy him, as his answers though very respectful, gave no elucidation of the mystery which shrouded them.

After remaining in the village for several weeks, she hired a house, or rather a hut, built on a wild romantic site about two miles distant. It was a deep gloomy dell, inclosed on two sides by precipices, which appeared as if they had been caused by some convulsion of nature. At the bottom there ever laughed a small murmuring rivulet, which issued from a spring farther up in the glen. Around the house, which was partly up one of the cliffs, the underwood and trees were cleared away, allowing the sun to penetrate into the darkness of the lone, wild spot. The tops of the cliff, as well as the dell above and below, were covered with a close evergreen forest.

After completing her arrangements, she removed to her house, secluding herself from all intercourse with the inhabitants. Whatever communication was necessary, was done by Legrand; and although their previous history still remained a matter of speculation and comment, yet their present movements had ceased to excite any curiosity. Her name had never been known, but she had gained the appellation of "The Mountain Woman."

Legrand had no other name, excepting sometimes the young ladies, desirious of evincing more respect, called him Mr. Legrand. The additional respect apparently weighed heavy upon him, as he soon began to avoid the society of his companions, and became more moody and melancholy.

With Catherine, he had ever continued the same terms of intimacy which were contracted between them soon after he came to the village, while they were yet children. It was the first time that she had ever heard him call her Miss Marvin; and that, combined with his entreaty for her to stay, for a moment embarrassed her; but it was for an instant, and then she laughed.

"Miss Marvin, forsooth! and so, I suppose, I shall have to turn round and call you Mr. Legrand?"

"No, no; not that," and an expression of pain passed over his face.

"Well," responded Kate, "we will make a bargain—I will not call you mister, and you shall always call me Kate—I don't like to be treated with so much formality, for it seems like jogging my elbow to make me play 'the dignified.' But what is the matter, Legrand? I have not seen you for more than a week?"

"I have been out of the place, making some arrangements which were necessary before my departure, and——"

"You are going away!" interrupted Kate; "where?"

"Yes; I leave to-morrow. My destination is a matter of circumstances."

"And your mother——"

"She will remain here for the present, she says, and she gives no assurance of following my fortunes. I called to request you sometimes to know her welfare. I feel, that you have not that foolish curiosity about her that many others have; and from you she would receive kindness and attention if necessary."

"I am so much surprised at this sudden movement, that I do not know what to think. Why do you leave?" and she blushingly added, "pardon me, Legrand; I know you don't like questions."

"From every one I do not; but from you——" he paused, and then subjoined, "I leave here, because there is no inducement to remain, save the duty I owe one who has shown me the kindness of a mother, even if she owns not the title."

Catherine looked up in astonishment. It was the first time she had ever heard him allude to his mother, further than to reply to some inquiry concerning her welfare.

"You are surprised, Kate; but I do not know that she is my mother. Never a word has passed her lips to justify me in saying that I am her son. Previously to our coming here, we resided in a city where she lived as secluded as now, and her habits were much the same. Upon me she lavished every indulgence that money could procure; but as I grew older, I became more inquisitive, and the answers which I received did not satisfy me. At this time we removed hither, and for awhile the novelties of a country life banished the moodiness which I indulged, unless, indeed, my thoughts were aroused by some questioning—perchance, of things which I could not answer. But now, what is the use for me to remain? Here I am but the son of 'the Mountain Woman,' without an object or aim for life. My heart yearns for a sympathy which it can neither give nor ask. No; I will go out among men. I will act, strive and struggle for a name, and then—' he paused, but soon added, as if musing,—

"No; I know not who I am—but far off in the dim memories of childhood, I can remember one of noble bearing, who used to caress me, and of a playmate whom I called brother. After this, nothing distinct is imprinted upon my memory, until I remember of being placed in a school in the city where we used to reside."

'Stop, stop, Legrand," interrupted Mr. Marvin, who had come out upon the piazza without their noticing him, and had heard a part of the narration:—"You must not fill Kate's head with notions that you are a prince, stolen from his kingdom. Let all such nonsense go. Probably you dreamed it. At all events, be it as it may, it is for you to act worthy of a noble father. Yes; go toil for wha you desire to possess, and if you persevere, take an old man's word for it, that you will obtain what you seek."

The interruption was most opportune, and called Legrand from an overflowing of confidence which sympathy begets, and which he had not intended.

After a few general remarks, Legrand rose to depart. "God bless, and prosper you," said Mr. Marvin, shaking his hand, and immediately retired into the house.

"Have I asked too much?" said Legrand, turning to Catherine, "will you see her sometimes?"

"Yes," she replied in a low voice, holding out her hand.

He grasped it convulsively, for an instant; and then relinquishing it, they parted with a mutual "farewell."

CHAPTER III.

AFTER Legrand's departure, Catherine became quite a frequent visitor to the 'Mountain Woman.' At first her visits were received with cold and chilling dignity, and at times with vexation.

"What dost thou want of the 'Mountain Woman?'" said she one day to Kate; "wouldst thou pry into what the imaginations of others have made a mystery?"

"No," replied Kate, "I seek not to know anything that you would withold; but since Legrand's departure you must be lonely. Permit me at times to come and enquire after your health."

"Lonely! surrounded by the spirits of peace and beauty?" And then she relapsed into silence, as if in communion with unseen beings.

Kate humoured her fancies, never interrupting her reveries, until, at last, the "Mountain Woman" herself, began to evince a deep interest in her happiness.

> Within each breast there is a power,
>   That wakes the spirit's deepest tone;
> And sweetens e'en the saddest hour.
>   And fondly breathes, it's not alone.
>
> It gives to life its purest zest,
>   And blends each tone to harmony;
> It even makes the wretched blest—
>   It is thy power, O sympathy!

At one time, as she sat regarding Kate with fixed attention, she started from her seat, and placing her hand on the forehead of the fair girl, she bent an intense gaze upon her for a few moments, as if she would read the inmost recesses of her soul.

"Yes," she murmured in her low, sweet voice; "yes; it must be so. Thou shalt know deeply of sorrow. In thy days there is mingled much of the bitterness of life. The freshness of thy sympathies shall be blasted—and even thou, with thy merry laugh and bright anticipations, shalt learn the loneliness of a desolate heart. Would—would that they might obey me, and ward from thy pathway the ills that gather over it! But no—it must be; thy fate must be accomplished."

"Why do you prophecy ill to me?" inquired Kate, regarding her solemn manner almost with awe.

"Why do the winds blow? why do the waters run? why does the earth yield forth flowers and thistles side by side? why is beauty given to some, and deformity to others? Canst thou fathom His will? I but list to the spirit's promptings, and utter their oracle—not my own."

Her voice had gradually risen, and she stood with one hand outstretched, and her form drawn up to its full height—a slight tinge upon her pale cheek, and her eyes kindled with enthusisiam, she seemed like a spirit from another world.

"Who, and what are you?" said Kate, with an effort to say something to arouse her from the strange mood in which she was indulging.

"Ay," she returned ; " What am I? A light being thrown upon the current of time—a thing sported by the whims and capriciousness of this changing world ! Time was, when I was gay, gentle, and happy as thou art this day, Others felt the joyousness of my mirth, and were enticed by my lightsome glee to be partakers of my life-springing gaieity. But time fleeted—and then I became cold and proud, distrustful of the sincerity of all who surrounded me. Why was this change ? why was it needful that I should learn the sad lessons of deceit, hypocrisy, and selfishness ? Why was it necessary that the sunny light of my heart should be shrouded in the dark clouds of disappointment and pain? Why was the warm current of my affections chilled in the veins where they once thrilled with joy, and left to return upon the heart with bitter coldness? Ay; bitter—bitter has been my induction to a knowledge of human nature, human passions, and a spirit of injustice which is abroad, but not human."

As she finished speaking, she passed immediately out of the door and was soon concealed from view in the forest, and Kate returned home in deep thought.

In their subsequent interviews, she never again mentioned aught of her former life, nor even referred to Legrand. Still Kate believed that she heard of him, and once ventured an inquiry. She regarded her earnestly for a moment, and then, at if speaking to herself,—

"Is it so !" said she, in a mournful voice ; and then turning her eye keenly upon Kate—"Nay this is not wise ; when thou canst learn to track the course of the eagle in the air, then thou shalt seek to trace the windings of man's ambition.

———

CHAPTER IV.

To detail minutely each change in country life, where thanksgiving is an era, and where every party is chronicled, were too monotonous. We will suffer a year to elapse since the commencement of our tale, during which time, Doctor Parker had become a resident in the town where Mr. Marvin resided.

The year was drawing to a close, and a " New Year's Ball" was upon the tapis. Doctor Parker was absent ou a visit to his father, but was anxiously expected, as he had been appointed one of the " managers," and it had been decided not to issue the invitations until his return.

In the evening, Henry French, the son of a wealthy farmer in the neighbourhood, called at Mr. Marvin's, and the conversation naturally turned upon the anticipated ball.

"Have you seen Doctor Parker since his return?" he casually inquired of Kate.

" No," she replied, blushing deeply ; " I was not aware that he had returned."

" Aha !" interrupted Mr. Marvin ; " if he has come, the invitations will be scattered like grain in sowing time. By the way, Henry, have you secured your fair partner yet?"

" I have not," replied the young man. " I hesitate to offer my services where I most desire, for fear of intruding upon some one more highly favoured"— and he turned his eye intelligently and keenly upon Kate.

She sat with her eyes bent intently upon her sewing, as if that claimed her whole attention. Her lip was compressed, and then suddenly a smile crossed her countenance, and looking up archly, she encountered the gaze of the young man with mrry laugh.

"Well, Henry," said she in a tone of jesting raillery, "as you so much fear that the fair one of your wishes has engagements detrimental to your gallantry, what say you to escorting me to the scene of festivity? I shall want you to come with a coach and four milk-white steeds—servants in livery of scarlet and gold, that the splendor of our *debut* may excite jealousy enough to make you ' the favoured' on the next occasion. Nay," she continued in the same tone, "'don't wear that perplexed and doubtful look. There is no compulsion in my invitation—you shall have, in all honour, the only privilege a lady has in such cases—the privilege of refusing."

The disconcerted air of the young man was sufficient to have provoked the raillery of one less mirth-loving than Kate.

" Pardon me," said he, recovering himself a little, and attempting to reply in the same manner that he had been attacked ; " Parnon me, for exhibiting my surprise or rather pleasure. I had not anticipated so distinguished an honour as an invitation from you, and—"

"Dont go any further," laughingly interrupted Kate ; " your reply is a lady's invariable preface to a refusal. Do not subject me to the mortification of the remainder—it shall be understood."

" This is not fair," interposed Henry ; "you are making my stupidity suit the pleasure of your own wishes—jesting aside, will you make me so happy as to accept an invitation from me, " said he, lowering his voice so as to be audible only to Kate.

" In truth, kind sir," she continued laughingly, in spite of the serious tone which he had assumed' " you have redeemed your gallantry, and thrown yourself freely upon my generosity for freedom. To prove that you have not misjudged me, I will say that, not anticipating the distinguished honor of your invitation—"

" Will you answer me seriously ?" he interrupted.

Before she could reply, Doctor Parker entered, and the salutations of the evening and the natural inquiries suggested by his absence, entirely precluded an opportunity for renewing the conversation which he had interrupted ; and after waiting a short time, Henry departed.

" And was Mr. French's visit to you ?" inquired Doctor Parker of Kate the moment Henry closed the door.

" Indeed I cannot answer—I did not ask him," quietly answered Kate.

" You did not ask him ! I had not supposed that you did—but did he not make known the motive of his call, so that you could divine whether it was especially intended for you' or as a matter of friendship to the family?"

" I certainly cannot offer any reason for his visit save kindness. Perhaps you are in his confidence, and can assign some other motive."

" Knowing that invitations to the ball was the business of the day, I thought perhaps he called to secure your company, and would have learned the success of his errand, before telling mine."

" If you are in company with him in the [business, I should have been happy to have been informed of it before his departure, as I then could have answered you jointly, which I should hardly be disposed to do individually. But aie not company concerns in business like this, something new ?"

" Kate!" and the tone caused her to start, and in spite of herself herey filled.

" Come, come, Kate," interposed Mr. Marvin, rising to leave the room, " I shall not allow you to quarrel with Doctor Parker too—and to punish your perverseness I shall tell your secret. She did not wait for Henry to ask her, but she asked him, and I believe is out of humour for receiving the mitten."

" Father !" interposed Kate, in a tone of entreaty. He laughed and left the room followed by Mrs. Marvin.

" You asked Henry upon the same principle that I remember to have received an invitation in days gone by, did you ? That is, you do not beg invitations and then accept them," said the doctor ; and seating himself beside her, and drawing her towards him, he imprinted a kiss upon her cheek. As he did so, he hastily drew back, scanning her face earnestly as she averted it.

"What is this—why these tears?" he inquired in an anxious tone of tenderness.

"Oh, George," sobbed the fair girl, "I thought you were angry."

"Forgive me, dearest," he whispered, drawing her closer to him "I feared

you doubted my faith—my love. From you, could not bear it." And another kiss sealed the reconciliation.

And thus it ever is. Man must not be doubted. His asseverations must be received, like Holy Writ, in full faith and confidence. A spark of jealousy will enkindle his anger.

On the contrary, a woman likes a lover a little jealous. It shows her power, and gives an opportunity for the exercise of that tact and management for which the sex is proverbial.

No. 2.

The truth is, woman always doubts. When she has yielded the warm sympathy of her affections—when she has learned the rich bliss of love's tenderness—she has embarked too much, at venture, not to feel anxiously. She knows that love is but the episode of the man's life, while it is the business of her's. She knows, too, that he has more temptations to inconstancy —more causes to bring oblivion over his memory—and more resources to fill the void of affections desolate. Man never doubts the constancy of a heart once his own. Estrangement may come—distance may intervene—his own neglect may have chilled—nay, more, his plighted faith may have been given to another; still he believes his image cherished, and his memory a green spot in the secret recesses of a heart that has once throbbed for him. Woman doubts— doubts herself—doubts her own power. Man feels secure in the supremacy of his own omnipotent selfishness.

*   *   *   *   *   *   *

The ball passed much as amusements of the kind generally do. The ladies were animated, good-natured, and pretty. The gentlemen were gallant and at-tentive, and exhausted all the soft nonsense which their brains had coined for the occasion.

Henry French was there, accompanied by a sweet girl more renowned for her pretty looks and amiable temper than for wit or brilliancy.

And, by the way, wit is the most dangerous gift ever bestowed upon woman. It may make her admired, but never beloved. A witty woman is envied by her own sex, and feared by the other. Men seek for gentleness, kindness, and pliability in their companions for life. They ask for accomplishments. (We do not use the word as generally understood, but as expressive of a common signifi-cation. The particular variety which would be desired by individual taste, would be determined by the position, whether a wife was wanted as an ornamental or useful piece of furniture.) Therefore, after summing up the virtues, they ask for accomplishments, neatness, beauty, wealth, and an affectionate disposition.

The above list was once given us by an incorrigible old bachelor, who assigned as his reason for celibacy, that he never found the qualities in perfection in a unit, and that he could not possess the fractional parts, unless he turned Mussulman.

But to finish the ball. Henry inquired of Kate whether she "asked the doctor or waited for him to ask her." She parried the question good-naturedly, and kindly sought to win from his memory the *ruse de guerre* which she had practised. After this, although not formally acknowledged (for it seldom is in the country), Doctor Parker and Kate were considered engaged.

CHAPTER V.

ANOTHER year passed with its noiseless step—and were the hearts which had welcomed it in joyousness and glee, as happy and light to greet again the "new year?" Had grief, sorrow, or the mildew blight of distrust, changed or withered the glowing hopes with which the year began?

Time passes, and with it change comes. In this world—and the thought may sober the gayer moment, even while it brings a balm to the grief-stricken and saddened hour—in this world, neither joy nor misery holds eternal sway. Sun-shine succeeds clouds, and clouds often obscure the brightest gleamings of the morning sun.

It was thus in Mr. Marvin's family. The sun of their prosperity was now obscured as unexpectedly, as unhappily. Mr. Marvin had given security for a friend to an amount that would involve his whole property. The fluctuations of commerce, consequent upon the condition of the country, owing to the war then raging between the United States and Great Britain, had ruined his friend's anticipations, and the result was, the whole amount had fallen upon him.

It was one of those accidental occurrences, inseparable from an unsettled state of trade, which human foresight cannot avert. And thus, without any fault, without any failure of judgment or prudence—for the bond was signed before the declaration of war—he was left in his old age destitute.

Mr. Marvin was not a man to sink beneath the pressure of misfortune; and promptly selling off his farm and personal property, he was enabled to meet the demand. And then his next thought was for his family. Fortunately for him, his known probity and experience would have enabled him to procure whatever assistance would have been necessary to commence life anew. But before he had decided what course to pursue, his old friend Mr. French who was his equal in wealth and worth, came to him.

"I have been thinking," said the old man without any preface, "that as things have turned out so, and you have got to leave your house, you had better move into my new one, in the village. I built it on purpose for Henry; but I don't see that he has any notion of getting married, and you can live there as well as not. It is snug and tidy, and will suit Mrs. Marvin and Kate, I am sure. You will have 'justice' business enough, with the town clerk's office, to support you; and your cows and sheep can run in the back pasture—it comes down toward the house, you know."

Mr. Marvin in vain sought words to express his feelings—he only wrung his friend's hand. The other, with a delicacy which could hardly have been expected from one of so little refinement—(but no, in spite of his rough exterior, he had true refinement, that of kindly and benevolent feelings)—did not appear to notice Mr. Marvin's inability to answer him, but returned the pressure of his hand with equal warmth.

"Well, well, squire, that business is settled. You can move any day you choose, and Mary will like to come and help Kate put things to rights. How I wish Mary was as blithe and hearty as Kate—poor girl!" And he turned, and went off as abruptly as he had come.

The matter, so summarily settled, was soon carried into execution. To remove from the old house was trying to them all, but none felt it more than Kate, although she had many merry suggestions to add to their new abode. But after the excitement of moving was over, and they were fairly settled in their new house, she retired to the room wihch was to be her own, and flinging herself upon the bed, burst into an uncontrolled agony of grief.

Mary French, who stood beside her, was the very opposite of Kate. An accident in early childhood had rendered her a cripple for life. From the suffering incidental to her lameness, she had fully learned the lessons of resignation, self-control, and self-denial. Her heart was warm and pure as the gushing life-stream of love and goodness, but her staid, calm, and dignified manner might have been mistaken for apathy or coldness. She knelt by the grief-stricken girl and clasping both of Kate's hands in her own, waited for the noble kindness of her nature to awake before she attempted condolence.

Those two girls—what a contrast! One beaming in beauty and health, with the real signet of commanding intellect upon her brow, broken beneath the weight of adverse fortune. The other, deformed in person, pale and sickly, like the withering floweret of spring, bearing without a murmur her own painful afflictions, and willing to have taken the burden from her friend's sorrow. She had learned that which Kate had still to learn—patience, resignation, and humility. How insufficient are pride and mere intellect to support the reverses of fortune, or calm the rebellious heart under the pressure of affliction.

"Forgive me, Mary," said Kate, starting up as she noticed the silent commiseration of her friend. "I should not have afflicted you with this—but, oh, how can I help it?" continued she, bursting anew into tears; "all—everything is changed but you."

"Nay, Kate, you are unjust. Much is gone that has given a zest to life, but

your parents remain the same. Thank God for the blessings left, and do not abandon yourself to useless grief. Dear Kate," she continued, putting her arms around
her neck, "God wisely orders all things for the best. We do not feel this truth,
but the future will teach us that it is so. You have yet to learn fortitude, but you
have courage; shame it not at this house."

Mary touched the only chord which would have vibrated in Kate's breast to
arouse her. She had piqued her pride. Condolence alone would have weakened
her. Her religious feelings were a matter of intellect rather than faith; and she
felt not the conviction to which her judgment assented.

"Yes, Mary, I have courage," she replied, "and I need it now more than even
you know of. George—" and she paused, scanning Mary's face as a blush
deepened upon her own, "I fear, too, that he will prove a swallow, and fly with
my summer."

"Have you any reason for this distrust?" asked Mary, in a calm tone.

"You think so, too, or you never would have asked that question, in that tone,"
Kate hastily responded.

"But you have not answered me."

"No; there is nothing in particular of which I can complain; but still, there
is something. He is always in a hurry—some business, some patient, or some
excuse to be off."

"If there is aught to justify your suspicions, save your own sensitiveness, you
ought to be grateful to these misfortunes for your deliverance from his insincerity.
But as you have always boasted of your independence in these disappointments of
the heart, I hope you will show it, if necessary. But oh," continued Mary, in a
mock-tragic tone, "if you should lay it to heart, and believe no more in man's
sincerity, what shall I do? for I have always looked for a snug corner in your house
in my old age." And she continued in the same strain, until she won a laugh
from Kate.

Mary suspected, even as Kate; but she would not admit it, and only sought
to win her from her thoughts, but without saying anything to encourage her hopes.

Soon afterward, Doctor Parker informed Kate that he had concluded to return
and settle in his native town, as his practice would be equal, if not better, than it
now was. He added that as soon as he was permanently settled, he hoped she
would be willing to consummate their delayed union. With a promise of frequent
letters, he left her.

Days had become weeks, and weeks had become months, but Doctor Parker
neither personally nor by letter gave evidence of his remembrance. And rumour
told its tale of other engagements.

Kate grew sadder; her boasted philosophy of independence did not stay the
falling tears—and why? High-spirited, proud, and courageous as she was, she
was but a woman; and women will weep, even for that worthless biped, a faithless
lover.

Take these disappointments of the heart, and they are "pretty, pathetic, and
interesting" in the pages of a novel; but they are directly the reverse in real life,
to the third party. Men regard them the same as an unfortunate termination of
any matter of trade. They sympathise and condole as in a mere business transaction. Women make gossip and scandal of them. And there is no consolation
about the matter, unless you can get two young ladies—smarting under the same
wound, with a comparative degree of confidence in each other—alone, and let them
indulge in retrospection and reminiscences together.

CHAPTER VI.

THE sounds of the war, which had ruined the fortune of a happy home, drew nearer. Report, with its many tongues, told its tale of a frontier invasion. Party politics, which had almost divided families and friends, even in that peaceful community, were fast merging into the broad ocean of patriotism. Their own firesides were about to be invaded, and the question of war, or no war, was forgotten in the stronger one of defence.

It was a bright and beautiful Sabbath morning in September. The people had assembled for their morning worship, and as the minister was concluding the portion of the Scriptures which he read as an introduction to the service, a messenger entered the house, and announced that the British and American fleets were about to engage on the lake, and that the British army was within a few miles of Plattsburg. The report of a broadside confirmed the intelligence, and the congregation instantly rose upon their feet.

" Let us pray," said the minister, stretching forth his hands.

Mr. French, by a gesture, and stepping down from the deacon's seat, interrupted the movement. " Brethren," said he, as he gained the aisle and turned towards them, "let those stay to pray who will—I go to fight! who follows me ?"

In an instant Mr. Marvin stood by his side. And as they walked down the aisle, every man in the house moved from his place, and with a quiet but determined step, followed them from the house.

For a moment, those lips were silent from feelings too deep for utterance ; and then there arose a suppressed moan, with here and there a sob, and the whole congregation, women and children, followed their husbands, fathers, and brothers, into the open air.

After a brief consultation among the leaders, the minister ascended the steps of the house.

" Brethren," said he, " let those who are disposed to defend their country and their own hearths from the sacrilegious invasion of a foreign foe, assemble here in fifteen minutes, equipped as they can best provide ; and may the Lord of Hosts and the God of Israel be with and battle for you : Amen !" And the whole congregation responded, Amen !

Kate had not attended the meeting that morning, and it was with surprise that she saw her father come home, at that unusual hour. She looked at him inquiringly.

" Bring me my powder-horn and ball-pouch," said he, as he took and was examining his rifle.

" Has the enemy come ?" she inquired, tremblingly, as she obeyed him.

" They are at Plattsburgh, fourteen thousand strong, besides their fleet upon the lake, that is now engaged with McDonough."

Mrs. Marvin entered, pale and anxious with fright. " Husband," said she "let the young men go—it cannot be necessary that you should expose your life."

" Good bless you, my wife and child, but no man can do my duty for me;" and he essayed to utter "farewell," but the word was not audible, and the next moment he was on his way to the rendezvous.

The mother and daughter stood in silence, and watched the brave little band march from their sight, and then they turned with a repressed sigh towards each other.

" Oh, that I were a man !" exclaimed Kate.

" Thank God you are not," replied her mother, bursting into tears.

The firing, which at first had been occasional, had now become continuous.

" I cannot stay here," said Kate ; " mother, will you go with me to the hill above the old house ?"

Her mother assented, and when they reached the top of the elevation, they found it covered with people, who were discussing the startling intelligence which had driven them from their worship.

"Ah! Mrs. Marvin, is it you? These are awful times—do you think the inimy will be here afore to-morrow?" said an old lady, coming forward and addressing Mrs. Marvin, as she turned to gaze at the lake, where the smoke was distinctly visible.

"Well," continued the old lady, as Mrs. Marvin was too much absorbed in her own thoughts to reply, "I tell you what is best to do—we had better destroy everything eatable and then go off. We can starve 'em off, if no other way—I pulled up all my garden fruit before I came up here—I could not bear to think it was ripening for the British and Indians to eat."

Kate could not keep sober any longer ; and bursting into a hearty laugh, "What will you do, my good Mrs. Reed," said she, "if the British and Indians don't come, and you don't go off ?"

" My child !' said her mother, "how can you laugh when your father——"

Kate was saddened in an instant, and her eyes filled with tears.

In about three-quarter of an hour after the firing commenced, it ceased, and the suspense then was thrilling. The battle was lost or won, and which, it would be perhaps hours before they would learn, To those whose friends had left less than an hour before there was, at least, this consolation—they could not have arrived until the contest was decided ; and consequently their lives were safe.

"It is almost impossible," said an old man who had hobbled up the hill, " that we have gained the day—for I talked with the runner myself, and he said that the British ships were larger than ours, and that if they wished, they could destroy the whole of our fleet without coming within reach of McDonough's gun. And there was but about seven hundred regulars in the fort yesterday, when the British army arrived. The militia were pouring in fast though, and they may thank Henry French and the brave boys who went with him, that they did not take the fort yesterday." " Yes," said the old man, growing garrulous as he saw he was listened to. " Henry and the boys arrived there, and what do you think? the fools had left the bridge over the Saranac still standing! The boys went to work pulling it up ; just as the enemy arrived on the other side. They let 'em come on until the bridge was nearly half full, and a column pressing on in the rear, when they opened to the right and left, and Henry ordered a cannon to be fired right into their midst. They fell back and, then tried to ford the river at the shoals ; but our brave militia were ready for them ther,e too."

Kate began to tire of the old man, and whispering to her mother that she would go and see the Mountain Woman, she strolled off in that direction. Not finding her in the house, she clambered up the cliff, and found her seated at the top, viewing the scene before her. She pointed to the lake.

"See," said she, "the effects of man's injustice. It strews the earth and sea with the dead. It makes widows and orphans—it desolates cities, and destroys the gifts of benevolence—and yet, this is what men call glory! Men—they can fiight,

dso can a beast of prey. But it takes a man to reason upon right, and a noble one to dare be just when the decision is against himself. The time will come, when prowess will cease to be justice."

Kate was too much excited to remain long in one place, and she started to return home. She had gone about half way, when, she heard a shout. It was caught up, and hill and vale reverberated with the cry of victory !

CHAPTER VII.

WE chronicle the darkest days, the coldest ones; and those remarkable for any other unpleasantness. But who marks the pleasant ones, or remembers the peculiar beauty of the sunshine, or salubrity of the atmosphere? The good of life we take as a matter of course, as something to which we have a claim: our misfortunes we murmur at, and forget that life, at best, is but a mixture of good and evil.

Late in the fall, Mr. Marvin's only brother, a wealthy merchant of New York, arrived on a visit. He was several years younger than Kate's father; and although actively engaged in the pursuit of wealth, the pure ore of affection was not wholly lost in the baser matter of selfishness.

Mr. Marvin had not informed his brother of the whole extent of his embarrassments, and it was with surprise that he had found the farm and property disposed of.

"Why, brother," said he, when he became aware of the true state of his affairs, "why did you not inform me of this? It would have been a matter of ease and pleasure for me to have rendered the sale of your farm unnecessary. Besides, if you were disposed to sell, your interest should have made you hold on just now, while real estate is so low."

Mr. Marvin replied, that it was better as it was: "I should not," he continued, "have much anxiety for the future, were it not for Kate. We have everything we want, but I am an old man, and——"

"Don't give yourself any anxiety about Kate," interrupted his brother; "I will see that she is provided for—and, by the way, you must allow me to take her home with me—a winter in the city will not be to her disadvantage."

"I don't know about that—it is a point on which you will have to consult her mother."

A consultation was held, but the question was not finally decided. Kate was rather desirous of going, but she had never been from her mother scarce a day in her life, and she was almost afraid to go. Her mother was decidedly opposed. Mr. Marvin assented to his wife's objections, but still he thought, with his brother, that it might be for Kate's advantage, and he rather wavered between the different parties. Moreover, he knew that his brother's wife was of a somewhat different temperament from her husband, and that at the house she was the sole acting partner of the concern, as much so as her husband was in his counting-room.

Kate consulted with Mary about the matter, and to her surprise, that true friend favoured the idea.

"It is not worth while, Kate," said Mary, "to deprive ourselves of a permanent advantage, because we have to sacrifice something of our feelings. We are in the world, and it is right to seize every opportunity to qualify us for whatever the future may give us—always provided that we do not sacrifice any present duty."

"But, my mother!" interrupted Kate.

"She will be lonely on your first departure, but after that, in the pleasing anticipation of your return, she will cease to regret your absence."

Mary was sincere in the reasons she gave Kate for her going, but she did not tell her all she thought upon the subject. One of the strongest causes which pressed upon her mind in influencing her to advise Kate as she did, was the conduct of Doctor Parker. She knew that the disappointment was too recent to have lost much of its poignancy in Kate's mind, and she thought that change of scene, new acquaintances, new subjects of thought, and a different routine of duties and employments, would naturally win so sensitive a mind as Kate's from a morbid indulgence of disappointed hope. And she thought correctly.

At length, it was decided that Kate should occompany her uncle. Before her departure she visited the Mounted Woman. After Kate had communicated her intention of leaving home, she sat for a few moments in thought, and then fixing her eyes keenly upon her, as she was wont to do when she addressed her,—

"You go," said she, "but you go weary-hearted—the light of your eye is not so brilliant as it was wont to be—you are sad, but not sickened with the heartlessness of man—you go, and you will learn deeper of the deceit, hypocrisy, and selfishness of the world. You will lose the trust and confidence of youth, and perchance its truthfulness also. Amid scenes of splendour, surrounded by the dazzling flatteries of fortune, you will feel more of weariness—you will learn disgust, and your heart will yearn for the sympathy which surrounded your humble home—but go ; it is your destiny—fate must be accomplished. We shall meet again—but where and when you may not know."

When Kate rose to go, she placed her hands solemnly on the girl's head, and with deep reverence, in a tone of benediction, said,—

"God bless, and protect you from man's injustice ; and the spirits of peace and purity attend you—we meet again—but now. farewell."

Kate's mother did not overburden her with counsel on leaving home. "I shall trust," said she to her, " to your own good sense to act with propriety under any circumstances in which you may be placed. It is impossible for me to see what may occur—consequently, you will have to rely mainly upon your own judgment. But, my daughter, we hope you will not allow any disappointment that has been, to influence you to reject everything unqualifiedly, which might be for your advantage. We should use our disappointments and afflictions rather as a warning and example for our future actions, than as a matter of despondency and disgust."

"My mother !" interrupted Kate, deeply feeling the tendency of her mother's remarks.

"Nay, my daughter," interrupted Mr. Marvin, who was present, " you should not seek to evade the point which your mother would come at. Your feelings at this time, perhaps, do not allow you to reflect coolly upon the subject ; but a woman should not, without reflection, reject an advantageous settlement, because her feelings at one time prompt her to remember the past more than to value the present. A woman can, if she pleases, learn to love a man whose character she respects, and whose personal qualities are agreeable. And we should bear in mind that, as the world is, a married woman commands a greater share of respect and consideration in society than an unmarried one of equal mind and character. It is of no use to speculate upon the causes— we know it is so—and that there is a greater prospect of happiness with a kind and worthy companion, than unconnected. We would not wish you to form such a connection thoughtlessly, and without any deeper feeling on the subject than merely to get married—but if possible, consider the matter as you would have done three years ago, and let the result be what your judgment may dictate."

"Let me assure you, my dear parents," said Kate, " that I will bear in mind your counsel, but—but—I don't feel it now. However," she continued with a smile, " I will try to be a good girl, and get married if I can. Like knights of old, I will start in search of adventure, and my adventure shall be—a search for a husband."

CHAPTER VIII.

KATE was almost wholly unacquainted with her aunt, and had yet to learn that one of the most prominent features of her character was selfishness. She received Kate with cordiality, as she had no children of her own, and she deemed that a lively playful young lady would make her mansion more attractive to the gay, than she had been heretofore able to render it.

She gave a splendid party to introduce her to their circle of fashionables, passables, and can't-helpables ; and as we have not much else to occupy our time, let us step behind Mrs. Marvin, and see who comes.

Mr. and Mrs. Blaight—the last on the list of can't-helpables, and the first to come. Good, honest, old Dutch souls ! it never entered into their heads, that they were invited merely because their fashionable cousin, Mr. Carlton, always invited them !

Mr. Grant, Miss Belden, and Mr. and Miss Grant. Mr. Grant is a merchant of the same standing in life as Mr. Marvin, and will come under the head of passables. Miss Belden is a downright, humpbacked, good-natured, independent old maid— a can't-helpable of the first quality—a sister of Mr. Grant's wife. She has, since the death of that lady, discharged the duties of a mother to the children, Mr. and Miss Grant. "Aunt Martha," as she is always called in Mr. Grant's family, fully understood her position in society : but that does not detract from her relish of the enjoyment of the scene.

Mr. and Miss Grant, son and daughter of Mr. Grant—or to speak more familiarly, "Lizzy" and "Dan" are fashionables, and a little more—desirables. That they will not go where Aunt Martha is not well received, will perhaps account for the very respectful attention which the good old maid elicits. But while we have been talking of them, dozens have arrived.

No. 3.

There are Mr., Mrs., and Miss Grafts—fashionables. Mrs. Strong, a widow lady, a passable, and moreover, a most intolerable gossip.

Doctor Sprague—ah, yes, you have come, have you? Doctor by courtesy—a a philosopher, something of an excentric, too. Neither a passable, fashionable, nor can't-helpable, is he. Rich, an old bachelor, amusing if in humour—one of those anomalies which we sometimes meet in fashionable society, we scarce know why.

Mr. Thompson, a young lawyer, something new—country bred. An agreeable fellow—but he has got his fortune to make.

Mr. Lee! there, see the buzz, the smiles, and every indication of being well received. What a puppy to make such a fuss about! As an animal, he is well enough; but a memorandum of his ornaments, dress, and so forth, would look like the advertisement of a jeweller, and barber's shop. His whiskers are exquisite; his mustache imperial; and he has chains enough to confine a maniac: see his hands—one, two, three, four, five, six, seven rings. It is a pity he has not one in his nose. Do you notice? his air is quite military. Oh, as the ladies say, he is a jewel of a man—who is he? The son of a man who spent his life in a series of contional meannesses; and at last accumulated a large fortune, and died soon enough to leave his heir and son quietly to dissipate it—for he has not energy to do it quickly. See there—pretty Ellen Crafts gives him her sweetest smiles, and her mamma is saying, " Pray have a seat with us, Mr. Lee."

Well, they have come single and double—in lumps and alone—until the rooms are crowded. Those whom we have noticed have prevented our seeing the rest on their entrance. Where is Doctor Sprague? Oh, there he is, right in the midst of a pleasant coterie of young ladies, with Dan and Mr. Thompson for rear-guard. Kate is there, too. What wonderful maxim is he now explaining, or what new proposition is he now advancing?

" A woman's life from fifteen to thirty has three district periods—that is, I mean an unmarried one. The married take colour, chameilon-like, from their husbands; and therefore, when a woman marries, she ceases to be, at least in the eyes of the law and philosophy. But the untramelled mind—the true species of the being we are considering—"

" Don't, doctor," interrupted Dan, " dont' refine any more upon the species. Let us have the result of your philosophic observations—what are the peculiar transformations of an unmarried woman's mind, as she progresses in life?"

" I was about to explain it. From fifteen to twenty, her life is one of hope of anticipation. She sees everything through the brilliant colourings of her own imagination. The vista of life looks but a shadowy lane, adorned by everything bright and beautiful.

" From twenty to twenty-five, it is all disappointment. The roses of pleasnre that she plucked, have withered. She is misanthropic—none of her hopes have been realized—and if she was naturally endowed with keen sensibilities, the way of life looks dark and drear; and perchance the only green spot she sees, is at its termination.

" From twenty-five to thirty (and you know an unmarried woman never gets beyond that age,) the world brightens to her. She is content to take the world as it is—she renovates her hope. The way of life looks but a short distance, which must soon end in— marriage. And at thirty you will find her as gay and as frolicsame as at fifteen, and perhaps more so"—and he turned his eye upon Aunt Martha, who was gaily chatting with some young gentleman whom nobody noticed, and who were too diffident to introduce themselves into the good graces of others, as if to illustrate his theory.

Dan was nettled at the look.

" Very ingenious, doctor," he replied;" "you should give the public th results of the observations of so profound a metaphysician as yourself."

" I am going to," replied the doctor; " I am going to tell Mrs. Strong—which will be publishing them."

"You may be profound, doctor," remarked Kate, "but we must not allow you to be ill-natured."

"And here is Doctor Sprague, the very personification of man's affection," said Aunt Martha, approaching the circle.

"Why so?" inquired Kate, suspecting Aunt Matha had heard the doctor's proposition on old maids, and understood his pointed illustration of his theory.

"Oh, they have several different stages in their affections ; but upon each you will find inscribed, like 'poison' upon the deadly drug in the medicine-chest—selfishness."

"Miss Belden is as complimentary as usual. As she undoubtedly has made man her study, as much as I have made woman, will you," he continued, addressing her, "enlighten us as to the progressive state of his affections?"

"I should probably make as tiresome a dissertation upon the subject as that profound metaphysician, Doctor Sprague, could," replied Aunt Martha.

"Nevertheless," said Kate, rather equivocally, "you will consent to amuse and instruct us, even as he as done—will you not?"

"Oh, do!" chimed in several others, who suspected Aunt Martha could pay him back in his own coin.

"You will find," said Aunt Martha, consenting, and seating herself, "that man has about four different stages of his affections. I do not know that they are confined by any particular limit of years. Sometimes you will find those who have no affections—their hearts are too adamantine to receive impressions. But to speak of the kind generaly. A man's first love is for beauty. His affections are bestowed upon the prettiest. Like a boy viewing tempting fruit, he desires it, because he wants to eat it. His own gratification, his selfishness, are the prompting of his affections.

"If circumstances prevent the possession of his first love, the second time his feelings are interested is for wealth. He still desires an objeet as gratifying to his taste as possible, but still the contingency of wealth is the ruling point in the matter. His desires now are to advance his position—to confirm his independence. Selfishness still is the master power of action.

"His third love is for ambition. Men generally, in their third love have made their fortunes—have proved their position in society. And now they desire an elevated connection, one that will bring them a step higher than their own exertions have been able to do. Their own aggrandizem ent is the object to be attained.

"Their fourth and last love, is for youth. They have lived beyond the active desires of life, and the infirmities of age are coming on apace, and they want a nurse. Their selfishness has corroded their life's blood ; but they are not willing to die, and they want a young and active nurse to fan the embers of decaying pulsation."

As Aunt Martha concluded, she glanced around the circle, resting at length on Doctor Sprague—as if to show the principle by which he was actuated in selecting youthful company.

"Good, good," said the doctor, who when pleased was very good natured ; "we have both proved our right to be called profound ; let us go and explain our theories to Mrs. Strong, and that will be publishing them for the benefit of posterity."

The evening passed off with agreable pleasantry, and Kate retired to bed at a a late hour, with her head confused by excitement.

CHAPTER IX.

"GAD !" said Mr. Lee, entering Mr. Thompson's office the next morning, "I thought something was in the wind, or Mrs. Marvin would never have given a party so early in the season. A country niece to be disposed of—pretty enough, but without the dowry of the rocks of her own mountains. However, she will do to fool with; and as we have nothing else to do this morning, come with me, and pay your devoirs at the shrine of this grass-green miss. Considerably smitten last night, eh ?"

"Nonsense," replied Thompson ; "I am always smitten with a new and pretty face. But come, let us see if the sunshine does not impair its brilliancy." And the young gentlemen soon presented themselves at Mrs. Marvin's.

Kate was not as brilliant as the evening before, but she was sufficiently animate not to disgust the able connoisseurs who were scanning her merits. They both came to the conclusion that she was passable, if not desirable ; her greatest deficiency was lack of wealth—for Mrs. Strong had ascertained and published her want of fortune.

"Well, Kate," inquired her aunt after their departure, "how do you like our city beaux ? Will they compare with your country gents ?"

"Oh, they far exceed our country lads in their fashionable attire, profusion of ornaments, the length of their hair, (and ears too,) if these are specimens."

"Kate !" replied her aunt, "be careful what you say. Mr. Thompson is a very fashionable young man, Mr. Lee——"

"Dont be angry, aunt," interrupted Kate. Mr. Thompson certainly made himself quite agreeable ; but Mr. Lee surely deserves the allusion I made. He told me of running over an old woman, driving tandem, and called it 'devilish fine.' He recounted a feat of frightening a lad in the country, and drowning his dog. He told me also of having stolen a market-woman's fruit, and gave me a long and interesting account, as the newspapers have it, of the wonderful properties of his boot-black, Peters. Besides he slandered every lady he mentioned, and proved himself a dunce or——"

"Nay, Kate," interrupted her aunt, "never let any one suspect you of ridiculing Mr. Lee. He is one of our most respectable young men."

"Why so ?" said Kate, astonished that she had made such a woeful mistake of character.

"Why so ?" replied Mrs. Marvin; "why, he is the wealthiest young man in the city."

The entrance of Dan Grant and Dr. Sprague prevented Kate's reply. Several others also called during the morning, and Mrs. Marvin was in ecstacies at the fashionable resort that her parlours would be during the winter.

A few weeks after, Kate accompanied her uncle to a public ball, given in honour of a noble victory achieved over the flower of the British army, which had landed in the south-western part of our territory. During the evening, as she was accompanying her uncle in a circuit round the hall, she became separated from him by the crowd. He was earnestly engaged in discussing with a gentleman the merits of the commander who had won the victory, and did not for an instant notice the separation. Kate retired within the deep shadow of a window, and waited for him to rejoin her.

As she stood partially concealed by the emblamatical drapery with which the hall was decorated, a young gentleman approached her, and in a light tone of familiarity addressed her.

"Well, my pretty miss," said he, offering his arm, "as you are alone, let me be your company ; and for your better acquaintance, we will have some refreshments."

"Sir," proudly replied Kate, "whom do you take me for ?"

" Oh, no matter who, provided you are pretty. Always where money buys entrance, there are many doubtful characters."

" Where is my uncle ?" exclaimed Kate, in a tone of vexation and alarm."

" Who is your uncle, pretty lone one ?" he inquired, with an evident sneer.

The tone piqued Kate, and taking a more perfect survey of her impudent insulter, she recognised the veritable Mr. Lee. The imperfect light could not wholly conceal the glitter of his tinsel. Mr. Marvin at the instant approached, and Kate sprang eagerly to his side. Mr. Lee stood still in the shadow, hoping that he had not been recognised.

Kate did not inform her uncle of the matter ; concluding, that if Mr. Lee was satisfied with the result of his gallantries, she would be also. And that gentleman had either too thick or too empty a cranium, to understand the chilling reserve with which Kate ever afterwards treated him. As he did not get a broken head nor caned back for the affair, he comfortably concluded that she did not recognise him.

The winter progressed ; and as Kate became an almost universal favourite, he began to contemplate very favourably the idea of making her Mrs. Lee. " But I won't hurry," he soliloquised ; " she will jump at the chance whenever I am disposed to offer it." His attentions, in the meanwhile, became more particular —so much so, that Mrs. Marvin began to entertain the strongest hopes that Kate, would secure the most eligible match for the winter.

" I think," said she to Kate one day, " that Mr. Lee's attentions to you are quite particular."

" I think they have been," replied Kate.

" Well ; if he should offer himself, of course you will accept."

" Certainly," replied Kate, " whenever I make up a collection of inferior animals of course, I shall want a monkey."

" Kate," replied Mrs. Marvin, sharply, " I shall not allow your country notions to ruin your prospects. Mr. Lee appears much pleased with you. and he is decidedly the best match in the city, because he is not dependent upon circumstances for his fortune."

" I care not either for him or his fortune," replied Kate ; " my country notions do not give me an inclination to be matched or paired with Mr. Lee."

" I suppose you would rather be an old maid, dependent upon the bounty of your relations, than to be the rich Mrs. Lee" sarcastically asked Mrs. Marvin.

" I shall probably be an old maid, but I will not tax the generosity of my relations much longer."

" You had better become a servant girl."

" I would rather do that than become Mrs. Lee," answered Kate proudly, leaving the room to prevent further remarks.

She sought her chamber in no very enviable state of feelings. The shafts of her aunt's matter-of-fact intimations and advice sank the deeper because of the desoation of her own heart. Until now,, she never had for a moment realised the degradation that dependence inflicts upon a noble and sensitive nature.

" My God !" she exclaimed, in utter abandonment of misery, " how dreary in the future ! The——"

She was interrupted by a tap at the door. On opening, a servant handed her a letter, upon which she immediately recognised Mary French's superscription. The perusal of the letter calmed her feelings, and she prepared to answer it forthwith, as requested.

She had a two-fold incentive for complying with the request : she wished to solicit something from Mary upon the *one* subject nearest her heart ; and she wished for her friend's sympathy in her present annoyances and trials.

In alluding to her aunt, her indignation did not allow her to speak in the most measured terms.

" She seems to me," she wrote, " destitute of every refreshment of feeling, regarding every relation in life as a mere matter of bargain and interest. As for me, she only regards me as a kind of ' country produce,' brought out on speculation. If she persists in considering her parlours like market-stalls, I shall suggest the propriety of her substituting turnips, cabbages, and squashes for ornaments, instead of the costly baubles with which she now decorates her rooms. As I am obliged to stay here until spring, I hope she will inform me whether I am considered a calf, a lamb, or a pig; so that I may know whether to bleat, baa, or squeal! I have almost cried my eyes out : but don't fear—I shall no more do so—I am too vexed for that."

This ludicrous view on the subject had excited her mirth, and between that and her indignation, there was not much cause to fear that she would ponder upon the matter seriously.

It is but justice to Mrs. Marvin to state that she was totally unaware of Kate's previous engagement and subsequent disappointment. But at the same time, had she been informed of it, she would not have pursued a different course, as she would have deemed a new beau the best medicine in the world to drive an old one out of the head.

After Kate left the room, Mrs. Marvin regretted her precipitancy in the affair.

" I ought to have waited," said she to herself " and let matters progressed of themselves. But of late she has appeared quite pleased with Dan Grant, and it would be folly for her to take him if she can get Lee. I know Dan is well enough, but he is dependent upon his father. Girls are always fools in such affairs. They don't know what is for their own good. But I must make her forget what I have said this morning, or she will take it into her head to be going home. What nonsense ; I have no patience with the girl !" and she went on planning and scheming, as if there was no power in heaven or earth that could defeat her purposes.

CHAPTER X.

KATE finished her letter to Mary, and wishing fully to recover herself before she met her aunt, she started to take it to the post office herself. It was the busy hour of morning, and a fashionable hour for promenade, and the streets were literally crowded.

As she was passing a toy shop a little boy, three or four years old, started from the door, and with an exclamation of delight darted into the street, apparently endeavouring to attract the notice of some one passing by. A gentleman put his head from the carriage, and ordered the coachman to stop. At the same instant, a horse with a carriage attached to him dashed round a corner but a few yards off. A suppressed cry of terror arose from the crowd, and Kate, wholly forgetful of herself, darted from the throng, and snatched the little fellow from apparently inevitable destruction. She placed him in safely on the walk ; and then a consciousness of the danger which she had incurred flashed across her mind, aand a sudden faintness oppressed her, so that she could scarcely support herself.

The parents of the little boy, who had been the cause of his running into the street, instantly alighted from the carriage, and embracing Kate, plainly evinced by their emotion that they deeply felt the gratitude which their actions expressed. A gentleman who had alighted with them, briefly explained that they were Spanish, and that their ignorance of the English language denied them the power of expressing how strongly they felt their obligations for their child's preservation. He ended, by offering the carriage to convey Kate home ; and assisting her into it, followed by the Spanish gentleman and lady, they proceeded to Mr. Marvin's.

The act which saved the little boy's life arose wholly from impulse ; for if Kate had waited for an instant of reflection, she would have hesitated to execute the promptings of her feelings, and her aid would have been too late. But impulse, as it was, it proceeded from the highest attributes of humanity, and saved a fellow-being from destruction. It was the unaided, natural promptings of the spirit—and shall we dare say that every natural desire of the heart is depraved? that each impulse is evil? What act of crime and wrong was ever recorded that proceeded from the spirit's instantaneous, impulsive prompting—without forethought—in a moment of total forgetfulness of self.

The gentleman who acted as interpreter, informed Kate that his companions were the Marquis Ariezaga and lady, refugees from Spain in 1808, who since that time had been in South America, but were now returning to their native land.

The marquis and his wife were profuse in their acknowledgments; and when they arose to depart, Donna Maria took from her neck an elegantly-wrought and massive chain of gold, to which was attached a watch of great value, surrounded with brilliants; and flinging the chain over Kate's neck, said in Spanish, (which was rendered into English by the interpreter,)

"Accept this as a memento of one who can never forget what she owes you."

Kate put it back, saying that she wanted no reward.

"No, no—not as a reward," continued the donna, when she had understood what Kate said, "but as a token, which you must ever wear, to remind you of the hour when your courage saved a mother's heart from bleeding."

"But," persisted Kate, "so valuable a token looks too much like a reward."

"Is aught too valuable for the preserver of my child? You saved me my only precious jewel, and you cannot refuse the token that a mother would leave to remind you that now and for ever her prayers shall arise to the Virgin Mary that you and all that you love may be shielded from harm."

The earnest manner of Donna Maria persuaded Kate of the propriety of retaining the gift. . The marquis embraced her after the fashion of his own country, and with feelings too deep for utterance retired.

Kate's daring act made her a nine day's wonder. Every one who could frame an excuse, and many who could not, called at Mrs. Marvin's to see and talk *with* Kate, that they might be the more eloquent in talking *about* her.

To be distinguished for anything remarkable—a deed of heroism, a comic grin, superior mental endowments, a light heel, or clear complexion, is like being a six-legged calf. Everybody must examine it, to see that the superfluous parts are not stitched on.

The marquis and lady intended to sail for Spain at an early day. About two weeks after Kate's introduction to them, in one of their morning calls, the subject of their departure was referred to.

"Oh, I wish I were going to Spain too," exclaimed Kate, as the romance connected with that country presented itself to her imagination.

The marquis, upon being informed of the purport of her exclamation, with great earnestness pressed her to accompany them.

"Nothing," said he, "shall be wanting that is in my power to procure, to make your voyage and stay in Spain agreeable to you. If you will go, you will but add to the very great obligation that we now owe you, and it shall be our study to promote your happiness—not cancel our own debts—that would be impossible."

Then Donna Maria added her entreaties also. "Will you go," said she, "and be as my sister, and let me teach my little Carlos to love you, and be grateful to his preserver?"

After this their importunities were renewed daily upon the subject until Kate consented to accompany them, provided her parents did not positively object.

She immediately wrote to her father, and to her friend Mary, earnestly soliciting their consent. After drawing a most flattering picture of the marquis and his lady to her parents, she concluded by saying,—

"Do not say that I must not go. If I am absent from you, what does it matter whether I am in Spain or America? In two or three years at most, I will return. It is a long time to look forward, but short to look back—and do not say, I repeat, that I must not go, for I am so determined upon it, that even your commands would hardly be obeyed. In a few years I will return, light-hearted and merry, and (as novel writers have it) improved by foreign travel. And be assured, my dear parents, that neither time nor distance can change the affections of your own   KATE."

Pained as her parents were by the reception of this letter, they wrote to her affectionately and kindly, to win her from her "mad project," as they termed it ; but, if her resolution was unshaken, they bade her go with their blessing. Her mother was unwilling to yield even this consent, but, ever passive, she submitted to the sterner judgment of her husband.

Mary also dissented from the voyage. "But if you go," she wrote, "be assured that, as far as in my power, I will comply with your request, and be as a daughter to your parents ; but come back," she added. "Oh, that I had never urged you to visit New York ! You cannot fly from your own thoughts ; and is it not better to share what you call your 'wretchedness' with those who love you than in a foreign land ?"

Her aunt remonstrated with her warmly against accompanying the marquis and lady. She thought it would interfere with the brilliant prospects opening at home. "If we throw away good opportunities," said she, "they may not offer themselves again for our acceptance."

Her uncle, like her father, was more disposed that she should act upon her own judgment. And finding that her decision was to go, he immediately placed at her disposal an ample purse to defray the expenses of her preparations.

"You must take the whole weight of the adventure upon yourself," said he ; "and whether your decision will hereafter be a source of pleasure or regret to you, remember that you pursued the course of your own election."

Mr. Grant's family, all of whom had become warmly interested in, if not strongly attached to Kate, urged her not to go.

"What shall we do without you ?" inquired Lizzy.

"And what do you want to go for ?" asked Aunt Martha.

"Perhaps," replied Kate, "upon the same principle that I came to New York. I told my mother when I left home, that I was starting in search of a husband ; and as I do not appear very fortunate in this city, it may be well to extend my search to the utmost limits that I can reach."

"Instead of seeking for a husband," remarked Dan, who was present, "I should think your aim was to run from those whose first desire would be to secure your happiness."

"Perhaps it is," replied Kate, in a tone of cool indifference, changing the subject of conversation.

"Inconsistent girl !" mentally exclaimed the young man ; "at one moment you are all kindness, and the next as cold as the ice of your own mountains."

Soon afterwards, Lizzy left the room for her cloak and bonnet, as she desired to accompany Kate in a shopping expedition. In an instant, Aunt Martha, who was one of the most considerate of human beings, remembered some domestic care which needed her inspection, and left the room.

Notwithstanding the advice of her friends to the contrary, Kate was so charmed with the idea of visiting the place which her romantic mind had indicated, that she determined to go, and accordingly set about making the necessary preparatons for her departure.

In the interval that would elapse before the vessel sailed, she made up her mind to enjoy herself to the utmost of her power, to do which, with Lizzy for her constant companion, was no difficult matter. The contemplation of the joy Kate anticipated from her projected journey caused the time to glide away in one continued round of pleasure.

Her mornings were almost exclusively occupied in receiving or making calls, and her evenings were usually spent at private parties or public amusements. To record each would require more space and more time than our limits would permit.

At Mr. Grant's (it chanced to be upon the memorable first of April,) Kate

joined with Lizzy to play off some practical joke upon Doctor Sprague. They thought

> " Time has its honour'd customs, free to all,
> The proud, the rich, the humble, great and small;"

and as the doctor was very temperate, (in the language of the present day a " tee-totaller,") they ordered the servant when he served the wine, instead of the usual

No. 4.

glass of lemonade for the doctor, to substitute a glass of salt and water. Alek grinned at the thought of "massa Sprague's wry face ;" and executed his commission adroitly.

"I should prefer a glass of lemonade to this," said Miss Crafts, as she reached for a glass of wine.

"Take mine," said the doctor, gallantly offering the glass he had just raised. "Do not hesitate to take it," he continued ; "Alek will bring me another one."

"Just like t'other one ?" asked Alek, with a meaning look, showing his ivory. The black's inquiry caused Miss Crafts to raise the glass to her lips. As she tasted the contents, with an exclamation of disgust she replaced the glass, and sprang from the room."

"What is the matter ?" inquired the doctor, hurriedly.

"I guess the lady don't like salt," replied Alek, trying to repress his risibilities.

"Salt !" exclaimed Mrs. Crafts, "where is it ? It will make Ellen sick."

The doctor understood the trick instantly, and having some knowledge of the *materia medica* among his varied philosophical acquirements, he told Alek to give the lady a glass of clear water, made very acid by lemon juice.

"Acid !" said the black, not comprehending.

"Sour, you rascal—nothing but water and lemon juice ;" and he started off to find Lizzy and Kate, to apprise them of their failure.

In the meanwhile the doctor's prescription had restored Miss Craft's stomach from the nauseating effect of the dose intended for him ; but not so with her wounded pride.

"No one having any claim to be considered a lady," said she, " would be guilty of such a vulgarity. I am sure Miss Grant was ignorant of the matter, and it is just what we might expect from an old maid and a country girl ignorant of good breeding."

Mrs. Strong, who heard the remark, as in duty bound, repeated it to Kate and Miss Belden. Aunt Martha immediately sought Miss Crafts to apologise, but Kate, indignant at the sneer at her country education, refused to follow her.

"You may tell Miss Crafts," said she to Mrs. Strong, "that any lady may, with impunity, be a fool one day in the year ; but some have the faculty of being so every day."

Mrs. Strong of course reported the remark, and thenceforward Miss Crafts and Kate killed each other with cool civility.

The doctor made himself quite merry at the expense of Lizzy and Kate when he found them. To turn the subject, Lizzy proposed a game of whist, as cards were included among the amusements of the evening.

"I have not the requisite talents for a good whist-player," said the doctor.

"Why, doctor," responded Kate, "I thought you had a genius for everything."

"Genius does not necessarily imply talent," replied the doctor.

"And why not ?" inquired Lizzy. "Pray define."

"Genius is invention—talent, execution. For instance, it requires genius to invent the game of whist ; but it only requires talent to play it. Genius is the original causation—talent, the power to execute the task that genius has devised."

"Oh, well," said Kate, "then in that case talent is by far the most useful. If I understand you, talent may be acquired, and you are not too old to learn ; come, and help me beat Lizzy and Mr. Thompson ;" and she took his arm, and led the way to the apartment devoted to those who chose cards to kill time.

On entering the apartment, both the doctor and Mr. Thompson noticed a curtain of gorgeous colours, which concealed a niche in the room. Upon a small table in front of the curtain burnt a small antique lamp, which emitted an agreeable odour. The table was covered with a scarlet cloth, embroidered with gold, and a heavy gold, or at least glittering, fringe swept the floor.

"What is this ?" inquired the doctor, advancing toward it.

"Oh, that is the Altar of Fate," replied Elizabeth ; "dare you seek to solve its mystery ?"

"No, no," interposed Kate, "the mystery there solved is one that cannot possibly interest the doctor. It is one that would more deeply interest Mr. Thompson, for he has not become—and I hope never will—a frozen old bach——"

> "Lift this curtain, and thou shalt see
> Who is most beloved by thee,"

read the doctor, from a gold-embossed card which lay upon the table. "And so this is a mystery which does not interest me, is it?" said he. "It is the very question I have wished answered. If I could have answered it myself, I should not now have been a frozen old bachelor, Miss Impudence."

"Well, you can have the riddle told now," replied Kate indifferently, as she was arranging the card-table and seating herself. "The deity concealed by the curtain does not often tell a falsehood, but she will show you a blank."

"Whatever my fate is, I will know, if I can learn, who I love most. But first promise me, ladies, that you will not either of you rise from your seats."

"Don't be afraid of finding Lizzy or myself there—we do not either of us flatter ourselves that we possess your particular regard. But come—we wait your pleasure."

"First, I must learn the mystery that this curtain conceals," said he, raising it, and found himself reflected from a large mirror placed in the niche.

"Truth! truth!" exclaimed Kate, laughing.

"Are you satisfied with the solution?" asked Lizzy.

"I'll give it up, ladies," answered the doctor, as he seated himself amid the small shots of his party, and the laughter of the rest of the company. "I'll give it up; what salt and water did not do, curiosity has accomplished."

"It was not to fool you," responded Elizabeth, "that I hung my shawl up before the looking-glass. I only thought to keep the vain from contemplating their own perfections."

"Lee," said Mr. Thompson to that gentleman, who had just entered the room, "have you consulted the concealed deity in the question which she elucidates?"

"No," he replied, taking up the card and reading the distich it contained, "nor do I need to—I know what she proposes to tell without inquiring." And he looked at Kate languishingly.

"Perhaps you are mistaken, Mr. Lee, in the opinion you entertain," remarked Lizzy.

"Well," continued Lee, "I can raise the curtain, and see if it does not reveal her whom I worship."

"No doubt, it will reveal the only being that you do worship," remarked Kate. "But be careful," she continued, as he took hold of the curtain, "that it does not bark at you."

"You are savage to-night, Miss Marvin," said Doctor Sprague.

"I have not killed anything but small game," she replied.

"Worse, worse: Mr. Lee and myself only small game!"

"The lion wounded himself," responded Kate, "and I have not hit his provider had enough to make him run." But Mr. Lee did run, excusing the act by saying that he "had forgotten to redeem a promise to Miss Crafts."

"You are a queer fish," remarked the doctor to Kate, after Mr. Lee had left the room.

"If you think so," she replied, "I wish you were engaged in the collection of a museum."

"Why so?"

"If you were collecting the curious and wonderful, of course you would seek to secure so rare a specimen as myself."

"I would as soon have a powder-mine and matches in approximation, as such an intolerable coquette as you are about me."

"Oh! Doctor Sprague, mercy! you have broken my heart—do not grind the scattered fragments to powder."

"Miss Belden," said the doctor to Aunt Martha, who entered the room, "what shall we do with Miss Marvin?   She has been cutting and slashing without mercy with the javelin of her wit."

"I cannot suggest any remedy for the present evil," answered Aunt Martha. "But perhaps your philosophic research and extensive benevolence, may discover some way to secure succeeding generations from the annoyance of which you complain.   I certainly think it would be for your sex's peace, if ours were born without brains."

"There is not enough of them troubled with the commodity, to make it worth while to remodel the sex," responded the doctor.

CHAPTER XII.

THE marquis chartered a merchantmen to carry his family and effects to Spain, and in May, 1815, they sailed from New York for Cadiz.   For the first few days the wind, although not strong, was favourable, and Kate was highly pleased with the sublime novelty of the wide—wide ocean.   But the placidity of the waters like the passions of men, cannot be counted continual.

The wind changed, and quickened to a gale, and beat the ship from its course in a more southerly direction.   The increased motion of the vessel changed Kate's enjoyment to suffering.   Confined to her berth, solitary from want of society (for as yet she could not exchange thoughts, even if she wished, with the marquis and Donna Maria,) the days seemed endless, and the nights for ever.   The romance of a sea voyage is quickly cured by the sufferings of sea-sickness.

The marquis and his lady both rendered every service in their power to alleviate the irksomeness of Kate's confinement and sickness, but attentions could not relieve the nauseating effect of the vessel's motion.   And the deepest feelings of joy that ever animated her bosom, she felt when she was again able to go upon deck, and view the glassy surface of the unbroken waters, and the deep clear blue of the boundless horizon.   There was just enough of the air to keep the sails lightly in motion ; and the birds, which still hovered over the water, seemed like so many messengers, to carry back intelligence to the shores she had left.   Was a for ever?   And the thoughts of home, of the ties of sympathy and kindred, awoke it deeper regret than she had before experienced.   She now realised the selfishness of the wish that prompted her to leave America.   She repented—but she must suffer the penance of her own transgression.

Nurtured, as she had been, in the very hot-bed of affection, she had grown proud, wilful, and imperious ; and the more generous and tender feelings of her nature had slumbered within the deep recesses of her own heart.   She loved her parents and friends ardently ; but she knew not how much, until her deep yearnings for sympathy, for companionship—alone, as it were, upon the broad bosom of the Atlantic—aroused the deep tenderness which had laid dormant in her breast.

There is a strange mystery in the human heart.   We rarely value present possession, or the boon that has been given unasked.   We are looking to the future for something more desirable—we are seeking for happiness which we shall the more prize for the exertions used in obtaining it.   And not until the present has become the past—not until that which we had already possessed has departed from us, do we know how priceless was that which we have thrown away, or wasted.

The compulsory solitude of her own thoughts did more in correcting the faults of Kate's character, in a few days, than would have been accomplished in as many months, and perhaps years, under the guidance of admonitions which would have excited the rebellion of her pride.

Natures differ : some require restraint and coercion; others, to be left to the direction of their own kindly impulses.

In the meanwhile, it needed not a sailor's keen observation to know that the ship was not far out at sea, and that the gale had driven them south, in the direction of the Gulf-stream. But the gale abated, and the change of wind allowed them again to proceed on their destined course.

Two days after they had passed the latitude of the Bermudas, a sail was described in the western horizon. It was in the afternoon, and the breeze but sluggishly moved the ship, while the lighter structure of the stranger enabled her to gain upon them fast. At first, no apprehensions were entertained; but a sailor's eye is quick to detect the fashioning of the rigging and shape of a vessel.

"I don't like the looks of her," remarked the captain, after examining the sail with his glass; "she is too light and rakish for a merchantmen, nor has she the solidity and make of a war brig."

The captain ordered the United States signal, and then the Spanish colours, to be thrown out, but neither drew a reply from the stranger. "It may be,' said he, addressing his men, "that we have got a d——d pirate to deal with. If so, I am sure there is not a man among my crew, but is ready to defend himself and ship to the last."

A huzza was his only reply, and every man was on the alert to execute the necessary preparations for a gallant defence, if brought into contest. They all knew that if the stranger was a pirate, the cargo of bullion and valuables on board belonging to the marquis, was probably known to them, and that the rich spoil would not be allowed to escape, unless defended with almost superhuman valour.

At nightfall, a light breeze sprang up, and the captain ordered the course of the ship to be altered, hoping to escape the company of his suspicious neighbour. But the stranger, seeing this, immediately veered his ship round into the t ack of the merchantman, and started in pursuit. This explained the character of " the chase," and every exertion was made to escape, while no preparation was neglected for defence.

The marquis, who was constitutionally brave, armed himself to assist the crew. Donna Maria and Kate were desired to confine themselves to the cabin. But Kate was not satisfied with the restriction, and refused to comply with it unless means were given her for personal defence. She urged her importunities upon the marquis more by gesture than language, although now she could command many words of Spanish, and partially understood the replies.

"What would you have?" inquired the marquis. "You shall be defended to the last drop of our blood."

"I do not doubt it," replied Kate; "but I heard enough of your conversation with the captain on deck, to know that you suspect the pirate to be aware of the rich booty the ship contains, and think it probable that the enemy doubles your numbers. I but ask the means of protection from worse than death, should you be overpowered."

The marquis shook his head.

"Do you fear me because I am a woman?" she exclaimed; "here—my nerves are as calm and collected as your own." And she laid her hand in his that he might see there was no tremor.

"What does she want?" inquired the captain, who had entered the cabin.

"She wants me to give her a keg of powder, that she may blow up the ship if we are overpowered. She says she prefers death to being the prisoner of a pirate," continued the marquis.

"D—n it ! the girl has not courage," responded the captain. "What assurance will you give me," continued he, addressing Kate, "that you will not blow up the ship before all is lost, if I will give you what the marquis refuses?"

"Sir," replied Kate proudly, "if you defend the cabin until the last moment, I shall know all is lost when I see the wretches approaching us; and my own love of life is the only assurance I can give that I shall not seek death, only to save us"—and she looked at Donna Maria—"from worse than death."

The captain was so struck with the cool courage that Kate evinced, that he ordered the gunner to place the powder in the cabin. He, however, saw the disposition of it himself, placing it where it would be as secure as possible from any accidental shot; and when it was arranged to his satisfaction, he turned to Kate:

"I have placed in your power," said he, "the instant destruction of the ship and every soul it contains. Do nothing rashly, but if needs must be, be resolute. While there is a man in my ship able to stand, he will defend the cabin."

The marquis rather resisted the arrangement, as his eyes turned on his wife and son.

"There is more mercy with God," answered the captain, intercepting the look, "than with these hell-hounds."

When he reached the deck, he communicated to the crew the disposition of the powder in the cabin. "And now," said he, "let every man do his duty, and defend the ship to the last extremity; and above all, as you value your own lives defend the cabin."

The men received their instructions with cheers.

"And after all," said an old tar, taking his place by a gun, "if they beat us. we shall know that in the end they will be beat too. A cheer for the brave girl who is too good a sailor to think of yielding to a pirate."

And they gave Kate three cheers.

By this time the stranger ship had approached near enough to show her hostile intentions, which she did by pouring a whole broad side into the marquis,s vessel. It was returned with equal warmth, and the firing continued for several minutes without either obtaining any material advantage. The pirate. profiting by the lighter make of his vessel, and screened by the darkness of the hour, (which was rendered impenetrable by the dense smoke which enveloped both ships,) by a slight manœuvre threw his vessel alongside the other, and in an instant leaped upon the deck of the merchantman, followed by most of his crew.

The battle now became sanguinary. The Americans resisted to the last, but finally the remnant of the brave tars were overpowered by the superior numbers of the pirate crew, and those not already killed, were secured prisoners without the power of further resistance. They awaited their death, calmly and almost with pleasure; for they knew their enemies would also be involved in their own destruction.

The marquis was wounded, and a prisoner on the deck, but the gallant captain had fallen before the cabin door.

The leader of the pirates, over the bodies of the dead captain and several of his brave crew, rushed towards the cabin. As his dark and brawny visage darkened the door,—

"Stay!" cried Kate, "one inch farther and your death is as sure as my own;" and she pointed to the powder.

The movement arrested him, and muttering an imprecation in Spanish, he levelled his pistol at her.

She stood still and firm; not a muscle contracted beneath his growling look of rage—and though pale as death, her eye quailed not beneath his fiery gaze. With one hand she held the lighted torch over the powder, and the other was stretched toward him as if to enforce the command of her words.

"Tell him," said she to Donna Maria, who had hid her face in the cushions on which she reclined—"tell him to fire—but that my death is as sure destruction to him as to me;" and she pointed her finger toward some of the powder, which was trailed in a circle round the spot where she stood.

The donna comprehended her instantly, and repeated in Spanish to the pirate, the substance of what Kate had said. Kate had not for a moment turned her eyes from his face, and saw that disappointment was beginning to blend with the fury in his countenance.

At that instant a scuffle was heard on deck, and the pirate rushed up the companion-way. The noise lasted for a few moments, and the imprecations of baffled villany rose upon the air, and then all was quiet. Kate stood still with the lighted torch in her hand, and her eye riveted upon the door. The marshalled tread above told that the victory was won ; and the suspense was becoming intolerable, when the marquis appeared at the cabin door, supported by a stranger in the naval uniform of a United States officer.

"For God's sake, lady, keep your torch firm," exclaimed the officer. "You are safe." And they paused, as Kate, feeling assured of safety by hearing her native tongue, stepped out from her dangerous proximity to the powder.

Kate extinguished the torch, and turned to assist Donna Maria, who was busied about the marquis, who had sunk exhausted by his wounds upon the sofa.

The officer immediately exerted himself in securing the powder. Several minutes elapsed before anything caused Kate to notice the stranger, who stood regarding her with fixed attention. As the restoratives somewhat revived the marquis, who was faint from loss of blood and over exertion, Kate turned to the stranger to ask some particulars of their rescue, and to thank him for his timely assistance. On raising her eyes they met his.

"Legrand !"

"Kate !"

And thus, those who had been separated for years met again : it was amid bloodshed and strife. The parting and the meeting—how different!

CHAPTER XIII.

THE American squadron, bound up the Mediterranean, had sent the timely rescue. One of the vessels hove in sight at the time the pirate ship gave chase, but was unobserved in the excitement of the piratical pursuit.

The commodore, now deeming it expedient to bring his ship into action, had sent a detachment of boats, commanded by one of his lieutenants, to the rescue. The boats reached the ship a moment after the pirate crew had become victors. Shrouded by the darkness of the night, and the confusion of the moment, they effected their ascent to the deck. The pirates, taken by surprise, and thinned in numbers by the recent conflict in which they had been engaged, were soon mastered. A few moments sufficed to secure the prisoners, and to liberate the crew, and the officer of the expedition then supported the marquis to the cabin.

That officer proved to be Legrand, the companion of Kate in former years. To indulge long in memories at that moment was impossible, and after a brief interchange of inquiries, he returned to the deck. First despatching a messenger to the flag-ship for a surgeon, he proceeded to separate the dead and wounded. The captain and eight of his brave crew had been slain, and five more were wounded.

The commodore accompanied the surgeon on the return of the boat, and finding the remainder of the crew too few to work the vessel, he left a sufficient number of his own sailors to man the ship, with Lieutenant de Forest in command. He also took possession of the pirate schooner, and placing the prisoners on board of her, despatched one of his lieutenants to deliver her up to the American government. This vessel was never heard of again, having probably foundered at sea.

The wounds of the marquis proved not dangerous, and the other sufferers were soon enabled to leave their hammocks. In the meanwhile, Kate and Lieutenant de Forest (whom the reader will more readily recognise as Legrand,) were fast renewing old sympathies and recollections.

" Will you tell me," said she to him one day, as they were promenading the deck, " the events that have brought us together, and why I find you in the navy ? "

" As you are perhaps the only one, with the exception of my mother "—he hesitated as he pronounced the word—" who have any interest in the detail of the last few years of my life, I will comply with your request."

Kate looked up into his face with a grateful acknowledgment of his courtesy. For an instant, a gleam of pleasure illumed his countenance at the interest she exhibited, and then it resumed its expression of habitual melancholy or reserve.

Although his face retained the expression of youth, its contour had lost the boyish roundness of eighteen. His form, although slight and graceful, had acquired more maturity. His highly polished and elegant manners, combined with the graces of his person, made him a truly agreeable and fascinating companion. Kate listened to his detail with feelings that we will not attempt to analyze. As his version of the events which had transpired, was altogether too modest, we shall give the prominent causes of his present position, in our own manner.

Legrand (or as we shall hereafter call him, De Forest,) when he left his mountain home, repaired to Philadelphia, where his mother's banker resided. This gentleman was noted for his probity, and strict integrity in retaining any secrets connected with his business. To him De Forest carried an order for funds *ad libitum;* and from him he hoped to gain some information respecting his parentage. Money and counsel were cheerfully furnished, but upon the other point the gentleman was immovable.

" Shall I go out into the world without a name ? " said the young man, when the desired information was refused.

" You may assume that of De Forest with propriety," answered the banker; " it was your mother's maiden name. But it will give you no clue to your father. Her immediate relatives are all dead. She positively forbids me to reveal your father's name, and mentions her own for your adoption, if you please."

" She is my mother, then ? "

" Certainly, did you doubt it? And now," continued the banker, " what is your inclination ?"

" I had thought of the sea," answered the young man.

" The navy, or merchant service ?"

" The navy, to be sure, if a midshipman's warrant can be obtained."

The banker immediately conferred with the proper authorities, and being successful in obtaining the desired warrant, De Forest entered on board the frigate United States. Under the superior discipline of its gallant and accomplished commander, he soon became an able seaman and thorough navigator.

He had been on board little more than a year, when the United States captured the British frigate Macedonian. In that affair, he so distinguished himself for his intrepid bravery and forethought, as to win the particular notice of the commodore, who never forgot to reward merit.

On the transfer of Decatur from the United States to the command of the President, he effected the transfer of De Forest also. In the gallant affair of that ship with the Eudymion, he again distinguished himself amid a host of brave men. " It was truly astonishing (says an eye-witness on board,) to see the cool, deliberate courage and cheerfulness that prevailed among the officers and crew, in the face of an enemy more than four times their number."

As a reward for his gallant conduct in that action De Forest was promoted to the rank of lieutenant in the navy; and on application, was ordered to the frigate in which Decatur was soon to sail for the Mediterranean.

Devoted as his life had been for the last few years to the achievement of glory, his feelings and affections had remained almost stationary. No new impressions had effaced old ones ; and when he recognised Kate in the heroine of the ocean, the partially slumbering emotions of the past awoke in renewed and increased ardour. With his characteristic prudence, he concealed the intensity of his feelings, and waited to learn the state of hers before he committed himself by an avowal of his affections.

With Kate the matter was more complex. She indeed remembered him with kindness, and met him with a feeling deeper than pleasure. Yet she probably would have experienced the same glow of gratitude towards any other human being who might have rescued her from such imminent peril. That other feelings were not enkindled in their subsequent intercourse, I will not pretend to affirm.

Under the convoy of the American squadron, the marquis reached Cadz in safety.

During the last few days, Kate had evinced more reserve towards De Forest than in the former part of their voyage; and he waited impatiently to see if their approaching separation would not draw from her some expression, whereby to judge of No. 5.

the feelings she entertained toward him. He gained, nothing, however, from his observation; and he could have stood with more courage and received an enemy's broadside, than one word encountered of raillery, or even indifference, from her upon the matter.

The morning after they anchored, preparations were made for the marquis's family to "go ashore." Restless, impatient, and dispirited, De Forest continued to pace the deck, revolving in his mind "the sweet cup of his bitter fancies," until Donna Maria and Kate came from the cabin to enter the boat. A veil completely shrouded Kate's face. He hurried up to them, and after bidding Donna Maria a kind and graceful adieu, turned to Kate. "We have met but to part, Miss Marvin," said he; "may I hope that we shall meet again before another so long separation?"

She merely bowed her head without reply, as she prepared to descend to the boat.

"Will you go without one farewell?" he passionately exclaimed, forgetting for the moment everything but her coolness or unkindness and their separation.

"When separation is truly regretted, farewells are but painful—and when it is a mere matter of ceremony, the sooner they are said the better," answered Kate. After leaving the ship, she looked back once, and seeing him still standing on the ship's side, she waved her hand in silent adieu.

The second parting, how different from the first! Then, both acted from the guileless kindness of youth: now both were governed by policy and worldly wisdom. Is this what the schoolmen mean by "the meeting of extremes?"

CHAPTER XIV.

MORE than a year elapsed since Kate's arrival in Spain. From the marquis and Donna Maria she had ever received the most considerate and flattering attentions. They never ceased to remember the great obligation they owed her; and as they now could converse with her fluently in their native tongue, her spirited independence, joined to the strict justice of her character, won their love, as much as her heroism had excited their gratitude and admiration.

Thrown, as she had been by leaving her friends, upon her own judgment and resources, she had acted up to the high behests of her nature. And being entirely surrounded by Roman Catholics, and aware that her religious opinions were a matter of suspicion to them, she endeavoured by a strict adherence to the principles of justice, to teach them that truth, love, and charity were not confined to particular creeds and forms of worship.

As the friend of the marquis and Donna Maria, she was everywhere received with the most flattering attention; and her beauty, joined to the playful witchery of her manners, made her a star of no small magnitude. In Madrid, where the marquis had been called in his official attendance upon court, she was nightly serenaded; and abroad, each cavalier sought to show the most devoted attention to the "fair foreigner."

But to the most devoted tenderness she was insensible; and when rallied by the marquis, that she had lost her heart to their gallant deliverer from the pirates, she would answer, mischievously,—

"Certainly, I lose my heart with every fair or brave gentleman that I meet; and it has been lost to me so many times, that it has ceased to be a matter of inconvenience to be without it."

An occasional communication which she received from America, proved her not at all heartless. Distance and absence only added to the depth of her affections for those not doubted. And for him who had crossed the pathway of her young life, time, her feelings had long ceased to be those of regret. A letter from Mary French, which she received about two years after her departure from her paternal home, communicated the intelligence of Dr. Parker's marriage.

I really wish, for the honour and interest of Kate, that she had possessed a little less strength of nerve. I wish I could say that she had grown sadder and sadder every day, until the rose upon her cheek had become a blighted and withered lily. But as I am a veritable historian, I cannot give her credit for many of these "interesting" traits of character. Time had diminished the vividness of the regrets which she first experienced.

Alas! for the constancy of woman's affection. Alas! for poor Kate, in your estimation, kind-hearted reader. Not two years had elapsed since she left America; and the only remaining blight of Kate's disappointment was, that she doubted man's faith, and had no belief in his constancy, unless when tried by law or interest. She had found one faithless, and she had an intuitive dread that they all were so.

Believers in one unchanging affection—those who have gained their knowledge of woman's heart from pages of poetry—may say that she had not loved. This we dispute. She had loved; loved in all the trust and fervency of a first love. Had the object of her attachment remained true, she never could have known change. Even then (her belief to the contrary notwithstanding), could she have had proof that his affections were unchanged, that he was what she once had fondly believed him, she would have turned to his bosom with renovated love—with the warm and trusting confidence of earlier days. She had loved as she never would love again, unless it might be a husband endeared by the associations and sympathies of a conjugal union, with that full and undoubting confidence which throws its halo around first love.

Kate was but a woman; but with her versatility of feeling, change of scene, and pride of soul, her thoughts had been prevented from running in one channel, and dwelling with morbid sensibility upon one object.

"I am changed," she said, as she read Mary's letter. "Would I have believed, three years ago, that I could ever feel as I now do? No; not if I had seen it written in the stars."

It has been wittily said, that first love is like the measles and hooping-cough —a disease of the teens, to which all are exposed; and truth compels us to add, that it is much less harmless in most cases, with proper treatment.

To tell those writhing beneath the smart, that time and change will cure their wound would but excite their indignation. But usually, less than three years of active industry or duty will cure the wretchedness of disappointed love. I do not say that it will in every case. The temperament, constitution, and organization of human kind differ, even as flowers differ one from another. Many are annual, some are biennial, and a few perennial.

In saying that Kate was well received in the circles to which the marquis and Donna Maria had introduced her, we mean, that untitled and without wealth, she never met the chilling coldness of haughty condescension from the pampered many, who look upon the adventitious aid of fortune as the chief good.

In Spain—in America—wheresoever luxuries are esteemed before virtues—where animal enjoyment is more coveted than mental excellence—there will be found the aristocracy of wealth—their worth will be estimated by dollars and cents. And amid the society to which Kate had been introduced, to be a man, in the highest sense of the word, was not requisite for honour or respectability. That there had been one man some time—no matter how many centuries ago, the more the better— was licence given that all his descendants, through all coming time, might be knaves or fools, or both, with all honour.

Of all the humbugs that have claimed the world's adulation for ages, that of hereditary nobility is the greatest. The worship of golden calves is a matter more simplified, more easy of comprehension, than the worth of blood, when the descendants have lost all claim to the qualities which ennobled it.

In answering Mary's letter, Kate rebutted with warmth and feeling the fear which Mary had expressed, "that she would forget, amid new and novel scenes, her friends at home."

"Forget those I love?" said she in reply. "As well you might suppose that I could forget to breathe and live. Mary, you have never been separated from those you love, and you know not how earnestly, amid scenes of artificial kindness, the heart yearns for the sympathy of those friends it never doubted. We value not the confidence that true sympathy begets, until we stand alone in the glittering multitude, and feel that among the many who flatter and praise, there is not one to whom we may unbosom the inmost recesses of our feelings—not one upon whose bosom we could lay our head without distrust, and weep, if we would, to our heart's content.

"To punish you for your injustice, I should send you a song that I wrote for a little melancholy air that Don Sebastian (Donna Maria's brother,) composed. He plays it on his guitar, and I sing the words about seven times each day. Here it is.

"'I may mingle with the gay,
As the sunbeams lightly play
O'er the hill, the dale and tree—
But my heart is still with thee.

I may lightly glide along
Through bright pleasure's varied throng;
And amid the glad and free—
But my heart is still with thee.

When to flattery's witching power,
I may gaily give the hour;
Still my heart, within its shrine,
And my thoughts are, dearest, thine.

And when moonlight's faintest beam
Quivers on the fairy stream,
Then to Heaven I bend my knee,
And, dear Mary, think of thee.'"

CHAPTER XV.

Don Sebastian Castanos, to whom Kate referred in her letter, was not the most safe companion that fate might have thrown in the way of a girl of her temperament. He had studied every winding of the human heart; and to the fact that Kate was rather an unique to him, she probably owed her safety in his society.

He was specious, wily, and insidious; and with every appearance of frankness, would machinate the deepest mischief, and perhaps villany. Yet he was not all evil. Within, there was another man—kind to his friends, generous to his foes, and the first to relieve distress and defend the weak from other aggressions than his own. He possessed the component parts of both saint and devil; and as the influences by which he was surrounded prevented his being the one, the necessity of his very nature compelled him to be the other.

He was about thirty years of age, tall, and well formed. His complexion, the contour of his face, and his full black eye, were decidedly Spanish. But his manners and general appearance were a mixture of French gaiety and Spanish gravity.

He was singularly attached to his sister's child, the little Carlos. And perhaps it was to the ministering influence of that child, that the evil of his nature at times slumbered, and brought him back to the freshness and purity of his own early impulses.

At times, for hours he would caress and join in the frolicsome play of the child ; and then he would start, while an expression of pain would cross his features, and exclaim,—

"What would I not sacrifice, that my feelings might be again as pure as that child's !"

Towards Kate, his intentions were as honourable and kind as they could be towards a lovely woman, who was not his sister. There was much in her that commanded his respect, as well as won his admiration.

"I wish," said Kate one morning after a serenade (of which she suspected Don Sebastian), "that your cavaliers would remember that I am an American, and in the night sometimes prefer sleep to the most flattering compliments."

"It is one of our customs," replied Don Sebastian, "to tell that we love—that we adore."

"I know,' continued Kate, "that in most countries night is selected to tell that tale. But if it be a love of which the lover is not ashamed, why should he hesitate to avow it even in the face of the noonday sun?"

Don Sebastian sprung from his seat, seized Kate's hand, led her into the verandah, laid his hand upon his heart, looked up to the sun, then turned his ardent gaze upon her face, and said,—

"Lady, I love thee. By the sun, the moon, and mine own honour, I declare it."

"Well done, noble sir," replied Kate ; "but if your love is as warm as the rays of to-day's sun, it must be scorching, and I fain would escape it."

"And will you not accept the homage of my heart, neither at the midnight, nor the noon hour?" he asked, as he led her back to the side of Donna Maria.

"It is a sacrifice that has been laid upon so many altars, that long ere this, it must have been entirely consumed," replied Kate.

"Not consumed, but refined," he responded.

"No more—no more gallantry now," said Kate, putting her hand over his mouth ; "I want your assistance in something else."

"In everything," said he, kissing the hand that lay so temptingly upon his lips ; "it is yours to command my services."

At this moment a wild-looking woman appeared in the verandah.

"It is a gipsy," said Donna Maria.

Don Sebastian looked up, and an expression of pain contracted his features, as he rose to bid the woman depart.

"Nay, nay," said Kate, interrupting him, "let us have our fortunes told."

He hesitated for a moment, and then bade the woman enter, and putting a piece of silver into her hand, asked her if she would "tell the lady's fortune?"

The woman was tall, but her face and a part of her person were concealed from observation by a large, dark-green mantilla, that she wore over her head. She took Kate's hand, and examining it, chanted, rather than said or sung :—

> "Thy life has been brief,
> But the cloud of grief
> Has shaded thy brow and darken'd thy heart."

Then fixing her dark, eagle eye upon the laughing girl's face, she continued,—

> "Now danger is nigh—
> The destroyer's eye
> Has marked thee his victim by wily art."

Then again perusing the fair hand that she retained, she added,—

> "O, bright lady fair,
> The evil beware ;
> Its clouds would obscure thy bright natal star."

And dropping the hand, she again fixed her piercing eye upon Kate's, and with her voice raised, and her finger pointing, she continued,—

> "Then fly, lady fly !
> The danger is nigh—
> And thy knight is over the waters afar."

"Lost, lost, Don Sebastian; my knight is over the waters afar," exclaimed Kate. "Thank you, kind prophetess," she added, turning to the gipsy—but she was gone.

"Vanished!" she continued. "But to the interrupted business. Your servant Palo is an arch fellow. Could he be trusted to execute a delicate commission?"

"Anything that requires address."

"Will you lend me his services for the afternoon and evening?"

"Why ask the servant, when the master is at your disposal?"

"It is my humour to secure the most valuable."

"Cruel lady——"

"But Palo——"

"Both he and everything I possess are at your service."

"I am generous, and will leave you what you deem of the most value—yourself." And she escaped from the room.

We will not detail the service for which she had sought and obtained the aid of Palo. Suffice it to say, that she had planned a counter-serenade, in which divers unearthly sounds constituted the principal part; and that the project ended in silencing "the sweet airs" of the cavaliers.

Donna Maria suspected her brother had been foiled and mortified by the result. "Did you take a part in Palo's admirable serenade?" she inquired.

"Undoubtedly. I should be but too happy to do or suffer anything, however mortifying, that would add to the amusement or happiness of your fairy friend," he replied, carelessly, yet Kate thought with a little bitterness.

Kate was humbled. To beg his pardon, or tell him that she regretted her behaviour, she could not, and soon she retired to her own apartment.

She knew that from Don Sebastian, she had ever received the most respectful attention and kindness; and that he had ever been ready to contribute to her happiness, and remove everything in his power that might annoy her in a strange land.

And what had been his return? Laughing scorn and unprovoked ridicule.

"At least," thought she, "I might have treated him with more consideration, as the Donna Maria's brother, if for nothing else." And from that moment, she felt a deeper interest in him than she ever before thought possible.

What a mystery is the heart of woman! I have studied it long, and still it remains as incomprehensible as ever. It hath as many keys to unlock its secret chambers, as there are emotions in the human heart. And the mystery is, that what will open it to one, will close it to another.

To win a woman's heart, maid or widow, be directly the reverse of him who last held empire there. If he was all attention, be indifferent and careless. If he was kind, be severe. If he was all deference, be dictatorial. If he in everything consulted her will and pleasure, then always consult your own. If he was proud, be humble—if gay, serious. If he was sincere, be a hypocrite! If his eyes were black, call yours blue. If everything be the antipodes of the last lover, ten to one you gain your suit.

Not long after this, Kate received a letter from her parents, entreating her return. The request was couched in language that scarce admitted of a refusal, even had she been disposed to have given it. She immediately communicated to the marquis her wishes, and as it was uncertain when fitting protection would offer itself direct for America, he placed her in charge of an English officer and family, who were returning to England; and with pain she parted from the noble marquis and his amiable lady, and sailed for London. They felt even greater regret than she, at their separation. But consulting her feelings more than their own, they arranged everything in their power to render their passage agreeable, and did not pain her with solicitations to stay, but urged her return.

Don Sebastian was absent when she received the communication from her parents, and her preparations were so speedily arranged, that he had no time to reach Madrid before her departure, although the Donna Maria had informed him of the events that were transpiring.

Kate was almost gratified that it was so. She was satisfied neither with her own feelings nor his intentions. That she was not a Roman Catholic, she knew was an objection. And, besides, ever between him and her, in her own mind, there arose another form connected with more pleasing associations.

When she arrived in London, her only thoughts was an early passage for America. And she positively declined the hospitalities which the companions of the voyage from Spain would have pressed upon her.

After tarrying in London less than a week, she embarked in a packet for New York. Her passage was pleasant and agreeable, and after an absence of two years and a half, she landed upon the shores of her " own native land."

CHAPTER XVI.

She tarried for a few days in New York. Indeed, as Mr. Grant's family were all absent on a summer tour, and their return uncertain, she would willingly have left the city the next morning after her arrival.

As it was before the days of railroads, her journey to the interior was more fatiguing both to her body and mind, than she had found the voyage of the Atlantic. The last day was almost insupportable. The nearer she drew to the scenes of her childhood, the more tardy seemed the rate of their progression. Her impatience rendered the days, hours, and even minutes almost interminable ; and when they reached the well-known boundaries—when she could recognize each tree and landmark—when her home appeared in view, how her spirit leaped, and yet shrank sadly from the meeting ! What changes might not a few weeks have accomplished ! Were her father and mother the same ? In affection, she thought of no change ; but then, in a few years age might be deeply graven upon the face and form.

She left the stage at the tavern, and leaving her baggage to the care of an attendant, she hastened towards the cottage where she had left her parents.

Although she had recognised many familiar faces, she could not bear that any other than her own dearest, should be the first to hear the sound of her voice ; and accordingly she kept her features concealed from view.

"That lady steps like Kate Marvin," said the landlord as she left the house, " but I could not get a peep at her face."

It was a bright and beautiful afternoon, like the one when we first introduced our heroine to the reader, that she returned to the place of her youth. But a few years, as men count them, had passed ; yet how much had Kate learned ! Thus far, her life had been crowded with the feelings of half a century. How much more some persons live than others, in the same amount of specified time !

She reached the gate of the little yard that inclosed the front of the house, and she could not but pause to note how different, yet how familiar, appeared each object. The impressions of memory were those of childhood, measured by their own image. Now they were compared by other scenes—those of the imposing, the grand and beautiful. And was that little cottage, what she had deemed quite a capacious house ? She paused but an instant, and then with a bound she crossed the yard, and the next moment was clasped to her mother's bosom. Why should I describe that happy meeting ? The poet has said that there is joy in grief, and it is equally true that there is grief in the heart's holiest emotions of joy.

By the time the family greetings were over, Mary French was there. Mr. Stone, the keeper of the village hotel, thought that he recognised Kate, and his curiosity caused him to watch and observe to which house she went ; and when he saw her enter Mr. Marvin's, he knew that his suspicions were correct.

" It is Kate," said he, in continuation of his former remark ; and the news fled like wild-fire.

'Johnny, Johnny," cried Mrs. Stone, "run and tell Mary French that Catherine Marvin has come ; and when you come back, call and tell Mrs. Radfield too. And the good woman hastened to "fix up" a little before she went to see her.

The whole village was, within half an hour after Kate's arrival, in a commotion. An event of so much importance had not disturbed their equanimity since the fourth of July celebration. A little girl, who had grown up under their eyes, had been borne off into "foreign parts," and had associated with great lords and ladies—why, it was a miracle.

The greeting between Kate and Mary was the warm exchange of feelings that could have no doubt.

"And where is Henry?" was one of Kate's first inquiries.

"He is dead," replied Mary as a tear fell to his memory.

"Dead!" repeated Kate, scarcely comprehending the intelligence "when—when?"

"He died about four months ago with the typhus fever."

Their silent indulgence of grief and memory was interrupted by the entrance of Mrs. Stone and Mrs. Redfield. These were soon followed by others, and a stranger would have supposed, to have seen the gathering, that there was either a marriage or a funeral.

"I declare," said Mrs. Reed (the old lady who pulled up her cabbages and onions for fear the British and Indians would eat them,) "I'll go and see how she looks—but I'll warrant she'll be so proud since she's seen a king, that she won't know nobody.

Kate was too overjoyed to be at home again, to remember one unpleasant association connected with her youth, and she returned each welcome with the cordial frankness which evinced sincerity.

"Well, I declare," remarked Mrs. Reed after she returned home, "I don't see as she is a mite different. I should never have guessed that she'd seen a king or queen."

Mary remained during the night, and when they retired to the little chamber Kate used to occupy, she found everything just as she had left it. There was the little table, with its white cloth spread ; there the drawers she used. She drew out one, and there were the thousand little mementoes connected with the memories of her childhood and youth. One was a book the gift of Henry. With a saddened thought she returned it to its place. The next was a curious shell, the gift of Legrand.

"Oh, Mary," she exclaimed, "I have not inquired for my old friend, the Mountain Woman."

"She is gone. She went away about a year ago, as mysteriously as she came," answered Mary.

"I have seen Legrand. He saved my life the only time I have been in positive peril—" she stopped, drawing forth a little box wrought from curled-maple, with all the ingenuity of a village artisan. It had been the gift of Doctor Parker.

"Well, Mary, you will laugh, and say that my love was but the evanescent beam of fancy. I have not thought of Doctor Parker until I found this. As I am well cured, you may venture to tell me of his welfare."

"I wrote you that he was married, and I heard last winter that he had buried his wife. He never has been twice since you went away. Once I saw him, and the other time I did not. He was more to be pitied than blamed, I fear. From some remarks that he made when I saw him, I am inclined to the belief that he did love you."

"No doubt. He manifested it most strongly by an unexplained desertion. However, I cannot be too thankful that it is—as it—as it is."

CHAPTER XVII.

DOCTOR Parker was one of those common compound characters, neither strikingly ood nor evil—one acted upon by circumstances, rather than bending them to meet

the behests of his will. He had feelings, sense of honour, and intellect; but he was a coward, and dared not maintain his principles or wishes, if strongly opposed. He lacked firmness and determination. His inclinations were toward truth and justice, but he feared to do right upon his own responsibility.

For Kate, he had entertained a deep and permanent regard; but from the moment that his father had become aware of his predilections, he had encountered uncompromising opposition.

No. 6.

"You! my son, marry that impertient saucy minx; I never will consent," answered the old gentleman, when consulted upon the subject.

That his father's prejudice arose wholly from Kate's laughter, the only time they ever met, he was fully aware. The partictulars of Kate s an swer to his father's interrogatories, he had heard from both ; and from the insufficiency of the cause, he thought his father must soon forget his resentment, if acquainted, with her naturally mirth-loving and joyous disposition. To bring them in contract with, out apparent intention, he now aimed ; and not to render his object the more difficult of attainment, he entirely concealed his father's dislike.

At this juncture, he returned home to live, hoping by acquiescing in one point to gain another. But after his return his wishes were more strenuously opposed than before. His mother joined with her husband, and their united opposition was more than he could withstand.

To announce aught of this to Kate, he could not. He loved her truly as eve —his heart had known no change—and he was well aware that her proud and independent spirit would scorn his subjugation.

Whether he was to be admired or censured, pitied or scornedwe will leave for casuists to determine. He had sacrificed the dearest wishes of his heart to filial a obedience. He also had deceived and deserted a trusting and loving heart, that confided the whole wealth of its tenderness to his affection and honour.

The conflict of his feelings could hardly be described, when he heard of Kate's departure from America. He had ever hoped (vain and fallacious comfort of the weak !) that something would occur to bring matters as he desired, by some other means than his own.

Bu now all hope of atonement for the wrong—of reconciliation—of an eclaircissement—was gone ; and yielding passively to the directions of others, he paid his addresses to a very pretty and amiable young lady in his native town—and but a short time elapsed before his parents, at least, were made happy by his marriage with the object of their choice.

Made matches seldom turn out well. We are far from affirming that every fancy should be indulged, without regard to reason or duty—nevertheless, inclinations forced—marriages of mere bargain and sale—contracts for duties and affections— almost invariably prove failures.

And thus it was with Doctor Parker and his young wife. Without any cause for complaint from either party, both were aware that something was wanting to render their union happy. To the world, they were patterns of domestic propriety. In private, they were respectful and kind to each other. There were no reproaches —no complaints—no angry recriminations ; but there was lacking that full and free confidence, which alone can secure domestic happiness. And in the second year of their marriage, either as a punishment or a blessing, they were separated by death. He mourned her—he regretted her death ; but still he could not conceal from himself that the event brought a sense of freedom.

Whether he had heard of Kate's return from Spain or not, was uncertain, but a few weeks after, he arrived in the village on a visit to his former acquaintance. The afternoon that he arrived, Kate was at Mr. Frenche's.

"If Doctor Parker be in town," she remarked to Mary, as she noticed a gentleman ascending the hill, "I should say that is he."

" It is," replied Mary, as he approached near enough for recognition ; " is coming here."

His and Kate's meeting had something of embarrassment to both, but she recovered her self-possession almost immediately, and commenced a light digressive conversation ; but had to support it almost entirely, with the little aid that she received from Mary.

He remained to tea, and evinced no intention of retiring. At twilight, Kate rose to return home. He arose also, and proffered his services to attend her.

"Oh no," she replied ; " you are well aware that your protection is not a matter of necessity, and I have a vow to be independent of all gentlemen's aid, unless the circumstances of the case render it absolutely necessary."

"And do you also exclude them from favours?"

"Not generally; only under particular relations," she replied, vexed at the interrogatory and its tendency.

"Undoubtedly, I am classed with those unfortunates who are excluded from grace; but let me ask from your benevolence, what I could not claim from your justice. I throw myself upon your mercy," he continued, not regarding Mary's presence as a barrier. "I would speak of the past. Will you deny me a hearing?"

"Doctor Parker!" she replied, warmly, "I will not evade a direct answer. The past, of which you would speak, has long ceased to be a matter of interest to me. I tell you this sincerely, to avoid further discussion on a subject which could not give me pleasure—nor, so far as I am concerned, could it give me pain."

"At least grant me one interview, and I will not trouble you further, if you request it."

"If it can add to your pleasure, improve the present opportunity," she answered, seating herself. "Mary has left us, I suppose, purposely that you might not be denied."

"I thank you for your kindness; and although my boon has been unwillingly granted, yet I must accept your condescension upon your own terms, and beg that you will listen to me patiently."

She bowed her head in assent; and he recounted the particulars of which the reader has been already informed; adding, in conclusion, that his affections had never known change—that his regard had never diminished.

"And must I believe," said he, "that you are all changed—that the past—that all the interest which I once flattered myself you possessed, has become obliterated?"

"You may believe it all," replied Kate, as she paced the floor. "The past to me now is neither a matter of regret, nor reproach—my only surprise is, that you should have dared to think otherwise."

"And is it a matter of astonishment to you, that I should have cherished the deepest feelings of my nature? or that I had some confidence that your truth and constancy were as unchanged as my own?"

"Would you reproach me that my affections are changed? Who first exhibited neglect? who manifested indifference? who, in the sight of Heaven and man, solemnly pledged his love to another? I may not have been true to you—but I have been true to justice and my own integrity."

"Kate! for God's sake no more. But may I not hope that your affections can be renovated—that years of devotion to your memory—that a life dedicated to promote your happiness, will again awaken some kindly interest in your heart?"

"Doctor Parker, this is useless; nay, more, it is ungenerous. You could sooner raise your wife from the peaceful slumber God has given her, than awaken one answering emotion in my breast. I did love you truly; but I have sought earnestly, even as I loved truth, to eradicate from my memory every vestige of that affection. I have mingled freely with the world—I have seen much of the distrust and hypocrisy that actuates the human heart—I have studied my own nature, and would sooner cast myself into the sea, than marry a man who preferred father or mother to me. A whole heart, and an undivided one, could alone answer the demands of my affections. And if I ever marry, it must be one whom I never have doubted—and one also who would not fear to do me justice openly and promptly, although the whole powers of earth were combined in opposition. I have answered you fully and freely, and it is unnecessary to prolong the interview. But first allow me to say, that your conduct towards me is not treasured as a matter of regret or reproach, and that there is not a sentiment in my heart but wishes that you might be happy. Adieu!" and she turned to leave the room.

"Stay, but for one moment," he entreated, in ce cked with emotion; "must this be? must all be but as——"

"No more—no more," she interrupted.

"I will not trespass, only to say how fervently I desire your happiness—God bless you, Kate, and"—but his voice faltered, and seizing his hat, he left the house. They never met again.

CHAPTER XVIII.

LITTLE more than a year after Kate's return, she received a letter from the Marquis of Ariezaga and Donna Maria, which changed—strangely changed the propects of the future. The letter communicated the intelligence of Don Sebastian's death, and that, as his last will and testament, he had bequeathed to Kate the whole of his South American possessions.

"Yes, brother is dead," wrote Donna Maria, "and he died by an assassin's hand. No cause can be given for the atrocious deed. He was stabbed by an unknown hand, as we left the theatre, whither he had accompanied me; and in the confusion of the moment the assassin escaped. He lived two days after he was wounded, and that time exhibited his noble nature.

"Much of his conversation was of you. You will remember that you did not see him before you left for America. When he returned, we saw that he was deepy chagrined and disappointed, that you had departed before he had arrived; but he did not communicate to us the bitter-feelings of regret which he felt. That was left for a death-bed to unveil. And whatever might have been your feelings towards him living, I feel that they will be regret for his untimely end and respect for his memory now that he is no more.

"He begged me, in his last moments, to write to you in his name, assuring you that the deep devotion which he was wont to express in the light tone of gallantry was but the faithful expression of his heart. He said that words could scarce convey the expression of his deep and lasting attachment to you. If he had lived, it was his intention to follow you to America and win your affection, if within his power. He thought that your feelings towards him were those of indifference, and that conviction only had detered him from the offer of his hand in terms that could not fail to convince you of his sincerity.

"As a token of his deep regard—a memento that shall keep his name from being consigned to oblivion by you, he begged you to accept his plantations in Peru; and he added if you retained the last kindly feeling to his memory, you could not refuse to take them as the gift of a dying brother, whose latest prayer should be for your happiness.

"And now, sister of my soul, that I have executed this commission—have communicated the intelligence of dear Sebastian's death, let me entreat you to come and soothe my bereaved heart. I know your parents' claims are first, but are not mind next? My grief surely has a claim upon your love. Will you come? if note, write by the next packet."

"Carlos is well, and says (as you taught him in English,) will my Kate come? Brother entailed his estates in this country upon my eldest son."

The marquis added that the necessary conveyances of the estate, with the king's confirmation to make the deeds valid, were forwarded through the house of the Messrs Rothschild, London, directed to the care of her uncle in New York.

The communication greatly excited Kate's feelings. The noble generosity of Don Sebastian his love and untimely death, could not fail to produce a tone of deep regret and melancholy. She mourned him, and blamed herself while she remembered the untiring kindness which he ever exhibited towards her, even in her most wayward mode.

She was unacquainted with the magnificence of the legacy, until informed by her uncle. A few days after, she received a communication from him, and pafter detailing the necessary instructions for her to avail herself of the income of the property, he added that it was worth two hundred thousand dollars.

"While we live," said her father, when informed that Donna Maria requested Kate to return to Spain, "my child, you will not again leave us, for a foreign residence?"

"No," she replied, " if you do not wish it ; my parents are first in my heart, as well as the first to whom I owe duty."

The acquisition of princely wealth humbled, rather than elated, Kate. To all she paid more attention, more kindness, than she had been wont to do before. And to the poor, and to the woe-stricken, she became the ministering angel of love and charity.

"To me," she replied, when reproved for her almost prodigal benevolence, "wealth has no charms, but that I can relieve want and alleviate sorrow."

"But some of your gifts, I fear," answered her father, "have created wants. I know the purity of your intention, but we should be wise as well as benovolent, in distributing the surplus means committed to our care by an all wise Providence."

The ensuing autumn, it became necessary for Kate to visit New York, for the transaction of some business connected with Don Sebastian's rich bequest.

"I would spend the winter there," she said, " if you, my father and mother, and Mary would go with me. When it was but a matter of choice—a country residence for summer and one in the city for winter, will you go with me?"

At first her parents demurred at granting her request, but her solicitations prevailed, and both they and Mary accompanied her to the city.

The winter passed agreeably to them and to Kate, so far as her reproaches of herself allowed her to enjoy it. She could not erase from her mind the impression that she had done Sebastian wrong. She refused all solicitations to enter society generally, and only received the company of her more intimate friends. This cirle scarcely extended beyond her uncle and aunt, Mr. Grant's family, and Dr. Sprague. Mr. Thompson was also sometimes invited to join them. With Lizzy and Mary time could not hang wearily, and almost imperceptibly the winter passed.

In the spring they again returned to the country, and wherever she went, she was followed by the blessings of those who needed aid.

As the summer progressed, she began to regain her wonted buoyancy. Hers was too glad a nature to mourn always, and not reciprocate the joyousness that was around her. From the Donna Maria she received a communication, acquiescing in her decision to remain with her parents, yet fondly breathing the spirit and confidence of affection. She added that the murderer of Don Sebastian had been discovered and punished, and that it was a woman, who had been maddened by a wild passion conceived for her brother.

This was the tale which had been told the donna, but the marquis knew of other particulars.

A year previously to the marquis's return—and consequently, before Kate visited Spain—Don Sebastian, as a pastime of pleasure, had won the love of a young and beautiful girl of gipsy descent. She loved him with all the wild and vehement nature of her race, while to him it was but the dalliance of the moment.

Soon after their return he left her; and as the association of his sister somewhat corrected the evil impulses of his nature, and the passion which he conceived for Kate rendered him insensible to the wild attraction of Kala's love, he refused to see her. This maddened her to frenzy, and she swore that she would kill the proud and foreign rival who had robbed her of his affections.

One of the tribe, whom Don Sebastian had saved from a cruel punishment for a petty crime, wishing to save him from the grief of causing Kate's death, and not doubting but that he would love Kala again if her rival was removed, sought to warn her of the impending danger, and remove her from Don Sebastian's society. Hence the wild and mystical warning which she had given Kate, when requested to tell her fortune.

But it would have been useless, and she would have been sacrificed to the gipsy girl's jealousy, had no other circumstances intervened to save her from the fate that the crimes of others were weaving about her. Her departure from Spain had disappointed Kala's threatened vengeance ; and finding the removal of her rival in his affections did not bring him back to the allegiance which she claimed, her love turned to hatred and revenge, and she sacrificed him to the fury of her passions.

Wrong—selfish wrong against the rights of a fellow-creature, will meet its desert and punishment, even if repented of.

CHAPTER XIX.

The succeeding winter, Kate, accompanied by her parents, again returned to New York; and she again mixed in the fashionable society of the world. Her greatest fault was in running to extremes. In popular phrase, "she did nothing by halves." If she mourned, it was deeply—if she laughed, it was heartily—and when she became the votary of fashion or amusement, she did it with all her heart. There were, indeed, moments of saddened memory, and hours of quiet retrospection—so that the giddy vortex of fashionable dissipation did not utterly destroy the energies and feelings of her susceptible mind.

As a star of fashion and an heiress, she could not fail to be followed, flattered, and have her caprices humoured. The one sex fostered her follies, and the other adopted them; while her aunt verily worshipped her, or rather her wealth.

Though a devotee at the shrine of fashion, Kate was not its slave; and if she willed, she rather led than followed its arbitrary dictates.

The servile subordination, in America, of all ranks and grades of society, to the fashion, irrespective of its adaptation to shape or complexion, has often been a matter of comment.

This winter, blue was the indispensable colour of the female costume. They wore blue bonnets, blue cloaks, blue dresses, and for aught I can say to the contrary, "blue stockings." The colour was not adapted to Kate's complexion, however she might admire it; and she appeared at a private ball, given by Mrs. Carlton, in a singularly rich and costly robe of Indian satin, but of a bright light orange colour. She wore a band around her head composed of rubies, fastened behind her ear by an exquisitely wrought gold button. The button also confined a superb black feather—its edges tipped with a golden hue—which fell over the back part of her head, and dropped upon her opposite shoulder. If she had met another person dressed in such outrageous taste, it would have provoked her ridicule, and undoubtedly she would have called her a yellow flamingo.

But her defiance of fashion or taste was generally received with the most flattering commendation. Those in blue were annoyed that their costume was not the latest style; and those who were in other colours, were happy that they had not adopted the blue.

Nothing is more annoying to the slave of another's taste, than to be defeated in not having the latest whim.

Doctor Sprague sarcastically inquired, "how long since she left her chrysalis state?" and added, "that it was rather out of season for butterflies."

Not long after, she was invited to the wedding of Ellen Crafts and Mr. Lee. They both disliked her, for neither of them had soul enough to forget the little things of past memories; but as she was the centre of fashion, it would have been inexcusable to slight, or even not to court her favour.

She accompanied Lizzy and Dan Grant, and both herself and Elizabeth were arrayed with extreme simplicity; but what was Kate's vexation on entering the rooms, to see her aunt decked out in a tawdry orange silk! and what was still worse, when the bride appeared, she too was arrayed in a dark orange colour. Ellen had naturally a pale and sallow countenance, and her dress made her look ghastly. There were several other ladies present, who also had "followed the fashion."

"A company of yellow birds," remarked Kate to Lizzy; "and the gentlemen in black dresses, we may call crows."

"You are to blame for all this," replied Lizzy.

"And so I suppose," continued Kate, "I must never be guilty of a folly, nor wear my night-cap wrong-side-out, for fear the whole world will copy my pattern. If they are such fools, I will make them all manner of birds before the winter is over."

This side conversation was interrupted by the approach of Mrs. Marvin, Kate's aunt. "Why, niece," said she (for she was fond of proclaiming their relationship), "why did you not wear your splendid orange?"

"I never would have worn it," replied Kate, "if I had thought it would have made a spirit-bride and a wrinkled witch." Mrs. Marvin, angry with vexation, did not reply.

"What a singular looking company we had last night!" remarked Doctor Sprague the next morning, at Mr. Grant's. "The butterflies have made their appearance so soon, that we may anticipate an early spring."

"Your evidences of spring must have originated in Miss Marvin's brain," replied Dan.

"True," rejoined the doctor; "and thereby is illustrated a favourite opinion of mine, namely, that the mass do not think, and consequently have no taste. The many are dependent upon the few. Discoveries are made and theories introduced, not by communities, but by individuals. It is the same in matters of taste and fashion : the multitude follow the leaders."

"You are very flattering to the ladies generally," remarked Lizzy.

"Not more so than truth. The leaders originate a fashion, or adopt a colour becoming to their own persons and complexions, and it is followed, without the slightest variation or adaptation, by others."

"Now, doctor," interrupted Dan, "you are getting into one of your sweeping lectures, and do not allow for anything but your own individual opinion."

"My opinion," rejoined the doctor, "I believe is correct, and founded upon impartial observation. I do not care how ridiculous a fashion the leaders of the town may adopt; provided it does not sacrifice more than half the modesty and nine-tenths of the common sense of the ladies, it will receive the sanction of the mass. Perhaps a few will prefer to retain their own judgment, but they will be sneered at, and called prudes."

"What a loss to society and taste, doctor," remarked Aunt Martha, "that you were not born a milliner, instead of a philosopher!"

"Probably! for as great powers of mind have been exercised to invent, construct, and adapt a novelty of fashion, as were ever brought into action by the invention of any novelty in mechanics," rejoined the doctor.

"Doctor, we must allow you to enjoy your own opinion ; for with you, we well know that an argument is but the loss of ours," remarked Dan.

"But I could give you a positive demonstration of the truth of my position.

"Which one ?" asked Kate.

"That the mass do not think, in matters of taste, any more than in the problems of science. If Miss Elizabeth and Miss Marvin will adopt anything that I may suggest—and I will not ask them to violate any principle of propriety, further than the adoption of some ridiculous fashion, some distortion of form or feature—I will lay a wager with you, that within six weeks it shall begin to be adopted by others, and within six months we shall find copies of it in all grades of society."

"Done," replied Dan ; "done for a wager of one hundred dollars."

"And shall I have your assistance, ladies?" asked the doctor.

"Upon the condition that we win the money, whoever may lose it," they replied. "And now, what is it to be?"

"I must have time to decide upon that," answered the doctor.

"Have the girls copy my crooked spine," said Aunt Martha.

"No, no," interrupted Dan, "not that. Our deformities of person, aunt, you know, do not affect the love and respect that our worth of mind and heart command from particular friends ; but—but——"

"But—but, Dan," continued Aunt Martha, "I know what you would say, but

—but, fear to wound my feelings. You think, moreover, that an actual deformity would not find admirers, and it would not be giving the doctor a fair chance. But so much the better for you, my honourable, sensitive nephew; and would it not be a deed of benevolence to bring your poor deformed aunt into fashion? not a follower of fashion, but the fashion itself? What say you, doctor? Your meditation is profound."

"What you have suggested is a hard trial: nevertheless, if these ladies have the courage to copy your 'crooked spine' (as you call the unfortunate deformity of your person,) and wear it for four weeks without either laughing at it, or telling why they do so, I will willingly lose my hundred dollars if they do not, in that time, find more than one who will copy even an actual deformity. Perhaps our fashionables will be slow to follow Miss Marvin a second time; but supported by Lizzy, it will take sooner. Ladies, what say you to wearing it six months?"

"Oh, I will promise to wear it a year," answered Lizzy, "if it will only keep strangers from gazing at Aunt Martha. Although she always laughs at the notice she attracts, I know it annoys her."

"And I will wear it as long," said Kate, "not only to keep Aunt Martha in countenance, but to see what docile gulls our dear fashionables are. If it is adopted, how I shall want to tell them where the last Parisian fashion originated!"

"Well, Mr. Grant," said the doctor, "the ladies and I have made our arrangements. Are you satisfied that it will be a sufficient test of the opinion I advanced?"

"It is too much," answered Dan; "it is more than I would ask; and I cannot say that I am willing that Lizzy and Miss Marvin should so deform themselves. Besides, I do not see what arrangement of dress they can adopt to give the desired representation."

"You would never do for a milliner, any more than for a philosopher," laughingly remarked Kate.

"The ingenuity of the ladies is far superior to ours, Mr. Grant," gallantly remarked the doctor. "But our dissertation has made me forget an engagement," he continued, looking at his watch. "Good morning. Ladies, do not forget that a hundred dollars is at stake."

After Doctor Sprague retired, Dan again endeavoured to pursuade his sister and Kate to abandon their wild intention.

"If," said he, after Aunt Martha left the room, "you are those to whom others look for just taste and models, your present intentions are a downright imposition upon the ladies, and not only upon them, but upon the public generally."

"Perhaps they might be," returned Kate, "if we had set ourselves up as the mirrors of fashion, but of that you will not accuse us. We—"

"So much the worse," he interrupted. "The favour of the public has raised you to an enviable position; and is it not ungenerous to abuse the good will which elevates us above another of equal merit?"

"No more preaching, my good sir," rejoined Kate. "If it be ungenerous, remember that the multitude sometimes needs a little correction, for want of thought and want of exercise of judgment."

"When there is mischief and not actual wrong, I well know that it is useless to dissuade you from its commission. But, Lizzy, you have not so many whims. Will you do this thing?"

"You are so complimentary this morning," said Kate, before Lizzy could reply, "that now I would imitate a dozen humpbacks for your punishment. So remember, Good morning."

"Will you, Lizzy," repeated Dan, after the door closed upon Kate, persist in adopting Aunt Martha's ridiculous suggestion? Nay, it is worse than ridiculous —it is culpably wrong. Will you adopt an imitation of her deformity?"

"Brother you are too sensitive about this. If it it were for nothing else, I would adopt it, to gratify Aunt Martha, although perhaps she did not intend us to act upon her hint when she first spoke, our willingness to do it gratified her. She does not realize how bad her humpback looks. But after all that ha ben se said, she would feel it, were we to decline copying it. Tnis, if nothing else, would give me courage now to look like a camel.''

"But surely we should not sacrifice right and reason, even——"

But the entrance of Aunt Martha interrupted him, and he left the room.

"Lizzy," said Aunt Martha, "Dan is so much against it, you must find some other method of winning your hundred dollars besides adopting my hump."

"Aunt," replied Lizzy, "leave Kate and I to make our own arrangement. We should not like to retract now. Dr. Sprague would call us cowards for ever, and Dan will get over his fret."

    *   *   *   *   *

Before a fashionable hour the next morning, Kate in her carriage, accompanied by Madame Bessieres, a Parisian milliner of the first skill, called at Mr. Grant's.

No. 7.

"Now, madame," said Kate, in continuation of some remark addressed to her previously to entering the room, "you understand me. A perfect copy of this lady's form"—laying her hand upon Aunt Martha's back—"the latest fashion, and in your estimation, it gives an elegant contour to the shape."

"Yes, yes," replied the madame, (as rendered into plain English for if we should attempt it, we should spoil her imperfect pronounciation, interlarded with French phrases.) "I understand, mademoiselle; the fancy is to accompany the orange satin."

"You must not remember that," rejoined Kate. "This is an improvement upon nature—nothing more. Remember, it gives a distinguished elegance to the form."

"Yes, yes, I know;" returned madame, apparently in a study, "but," continued she, "cotton will not do to shape it. Cotton will slide if pushed hard, and make it soft; it will be too airy—too light."

"Then what will do, madame?" inquired Lizzy.

"Flour—that is more dense," answered madame.

"Flour!" interrupted Kate, "that would be too heavy. Besides, it would sift out."

"Not the flour—not bread flour," rejoined madame, "but the coarse flour, the chaff flour."

"Bran?" said Kate.

"Yes, that is it;" answered madame.

Having completed her instructions, Kate retired with her artist.

Two days after, at a party given by Mrs. Marvin, Lizzy and Kate appeared with their improved forms. Kate's parents usually declined invitations to parties, but accompanied her to their brother's. Before they went, her mother, in a mild tone of remonstrance, endeavoured to persuade her not to adopt the improvement; but she was too much accustomed to following her own fancies to heed her mother's remonstrance. "Why, mother," said she, "everybody will envy us, rather than laugh at us, as you say."

"I hope it will be as you anticipate," returned her mother; "but certainly I fear you are carrying a joke too far."

"Not at all, dear mother," she replied; "you would not believe, should I tell you, how far an heiress and a belle may go."

Their appearance created quite a sensation; but at first, the voice of the ladies was rather against the invention. Kate supported her part with great *sang froid*; but Lizzy's brother had said so much to her, that she could hardly endure with composure the gaze that was rivetted upon them.

"Don't blush so like a school girl," said Kate to her. "Soon our novelty will cease to attract anything but admiration."

"I hope so," replied Lizzy, "but I cannot help wishing myself at home."

"Good evening, my dear Mrs. Strong," said Doctor Sprague to that lady. "What an agreeable company; and Miss Marvin and Miss Grant as usual, the most elegant ladies in the room."

"Why, doctor," interrupted Mrs. Strong, "there is something very odd about them."

"Odd! my dear Mrs. Strong," rejoined the doctor, "you mean distinguished elegance, not only in selection of dress and ornaments, but also in their peculiar arrangement. Such a perfect outline of figure! How meagre Mrs. Lee looks beside them!"

It was enough. His remarks, as he intended, were repeated to half the ladies in the room before the company retired, and before another week, Madame Bessieres was thronged with applicants for the new fashion! Indeed, their manufacture became a very reluctive branch of her business—so much so, that for her own interest she kept the secret.

Kate and Aunt Martha laughed; Lizzy could not help smiling; Dan paid his hundred dollars with a good grace, and thanked the doctor for the lesson—saying, that he had learned so much of the mysteries of fashionable dress, that he should be equally careful of trusting to the feelings of a fashionable heart!

Kate understood the inuendo couched in his words; and she had too great a love for truth, and was not enough of a coquette, to wish it otherwise.

Doctor Sprague received the success of his triumph with the quiet satisfaction of a philosopher. And the fashion had its day, and was laid for something else as novel, to be renewed and adopted in more modern times, improved—if increase of size can be considered an improvement

CHAPTER XX

THE next summer, Lizzy and Dan accompanied Kate and her parents when they returned to the country.

One of the first dispositions Kate had made of her wealth, had been the purchase of the cottage in which her parents resided. When Mr. French was applied to for its purchase, "Yes," said he, "that is right. When your uncle wanted to buy it, I would not sell it to him, for I thought I could afford to let my old friend live in it, as well as a New-York merchant. But now it is as it should be; and, Kate you may have it at your own price, and whatever you pay me shall be Mary's." We need not add that the price paid was generous.

The cottage had been repaired and refitted, but not altered or enlarged. It was not superior to any of its neighbours, save in its finished simplicity, and the extreme neatness of its garden and shrubbery. No ill-displayed ostentation proclaimed the wealth of its owner; but there it was, small, neat, quiet, and snug, half hid in its bowers of honeysuckles and roses.

Dan and Lizzy were charmed with it.

"Why," said Dan, "I had not anticipated anything like this as the retreat of the gay and fashionable Miss Marvin."

"And what had you expected, my grave sir?" inquired Kate.

"I do not know myself—but pictures and statues, and something of an European villa."

"What should I do with pictures here?" rejoined Kate. "There," she added, pointing to the landscape before them, "is one done by a Master's hand, and not to be imitated by the puerile efforts of man. And what statues could be in keeping with the scene, unless," she added with a laugh, "it might be those of a sheep and lamb; and having the originals we do not need the semblance."

"It is so different to your city residence," rejoined Dan, "where you indulged ing these things almost extravagantly. But here, everything is rural, everything as simple as a country maiden might indulge—nothing foreign, save these splendid exotics."

"Yes, they well show Mary's care," remarked Kate of the beautiful plant, he was examining—and then referring to his former remarks, "in the city," said she "and in winter one needs toys for amusement; but here, in the summer, they would be out of place. These influences are better;" and she pointed to the mountains, and the far-off lake, and the quiet valley outstretched before them.

He looked at her with astonishment.

"Miss Marvin!" said he, "after an intimacy of years, you are a riddle to me."

"Because I love mirth and gaiety, and then love nature more. But there come Lizzy and Mary"—and she bounded off like a frolicsome child to meet them.

The quietness of their country amusement was varied this season by the arrival of the Hon. Mr. Sumpter, and his father, from South Carolina. The gentlemen were upon a northern tour, for the benefit of the elder one's health; and, pleased with the beauty of the surounding scenery, they remained at the village hotel many weeks.

An acquaintance between the younger gentleman and Mr. Grant accidentally commenced in a fishing excursion, and courteous urbanity of the young legislator's manners, joined with his winning suavity, soon placed them upon terms of intimacy. Dan returned, and with animation related his encounter with the honourable gentleman. Lizzy and Kate laughed at him for his enthusiastic description of an hour's acquaintance. " I assure you," he replied, " that he is no ordinary man who could render an hour so agreeable, tormented as we were by flies and mosquitoes in the shade."

" Sumpter?" said Kate, inquiringly ; " the name sounds familiar."

" When we parted," continued Dan, " he begged my name, saying that his was Charles Sumpter, of South Carolina."

" Charles Sumpter, of South Carolina ?" repeated Lizzy ; " why, that is the name of the young member of the house of representatives, of whom my father spoke in such terms of praise when he returned from Washington this spring."

" Let me see," said Kate, musing. " His maiden speech was said by critics to be one of the most classical and eloquent efforts of a master-spirit. You will, of course, introduce us to this young Cicero ?"

" Certainly, if his pleasure permits ; but he told me his movements were regulated by the will of an invalid father."

The desired introduction was soon obtained, and the time sped swiftly as the weeks passed on, enlivened by the refined and interesting society of the young southerner.

Charles Sumpter had entered early upon the career of honourable fame. He had been elected, by an almost unanimous vote of his native district, to the office of representing them in the National Legislature, at the age of thirty-one. His debut the winter before had created a considerable sensation, and his subsequent deportment through the session had won the commendation of all parties. It had been equally removed from pusillanimous modesty and forward pretension ; and while he supported his opinions with independence and manly freedom, he courteously extended the same privileges to his opponents.

Mr. Grant, who had been elected two or three years previously as a member of Congress, was won by the superior talents which he exhibited in the council hall as much as his son had been by his intelligence and suavity as a chance stranger in the woods of Vermont.

While Mr. Sumptor was winning his way to the good graces of Kate, and her less whimsical friend, Lizzy, Dan thought that the whole responsibility of Mary, in their rambles and home amusements, devolved upon him.

" Have a care Mary," said Kate, one day when the gentlemen were not present, " or Dan will win you from your sublimated theory of living and dying a maiden."

" Oh, Kate !" replied Mary, as the tears filled her eyes, " would you make my deformity a matter of mirth ?"

" No, no, dear," returned Kate, caressing her ; " but I would give you a hint that these lonely communings with Dan may be dangerous to him, should you persist in the idea that your lameness disqualifies you for a wife. He loves simplicity and purity of heart, and I should not be surprised if he loved their personification in a sweet friend of mine, one Miss Mary French."

" At any rate," rejoined Mary, satisfied that Kate had not intended the attack unkindly " I should be assured that I only received a sacrifice that had been rejected at your shrine. You know that it is my part to gather up the fragments, so that nothing may be lost."

" Well, well," replied Kate, " if you have proceeded far enough for these considerations, my caution has come rather late."

" Not so," hastily rejoined Mary. " I only meant to return your hint, that I was aware you had rejected what you were so generously giving to me."

" We do not pay much attention to your presence, Lizzy," continued Kate,

' in canvassing your brother's intentions. But I have not done with my hints. You, too, have need to be careful that Mr. Sumpter's society does not become an indispensable in your list of life-items."

"You are very generous in your disposal of that of which you have no command," rejoined Lizzy; "I will profit by your hints when I feel that there is need of your caution."

"Have a care! have a care! that is all I have to say," said Kate, as the gentlemen entered the room.

"What is that you have to say?" asked Dan.

"That I burned my fingers once, most terribly, in meddling with a hot pie, not my own."

"I stand corrected," he rejoined. "But come, ladies, Mr Sumpter and myself are candidates for the favour of your company in a walk."

"As usual, I shall have to be pioneer," remarked Kate, when she returned with her bonnet, and turned to lead the way.

"Miss Marvin," remarked Mr. Sumpter, "is, I believe, one of those ladies who love to show their independence of those attentions which it is our happiness to tender them."

"Independent only in the country," rejoined Kate, looking back. "Here I feel it my duty to extend to you the hospitality of all the fences, walls, and ditches. Ladies and gentlemen, I pray you feel yourselves at home with these slight obstructions, and jump them if you can." And like one well practised in the feat, she set the example, by climbing a wall that obstructed their way.

"Why, whither are you leading us?" inquired Lizzy.

"To a lecture upon philosophy," she answered, continuing her way through a stony upland pasture. At last they reached the confines of a pleasant woodland, surrounded by a dense growth of bushes.

"Oh, see those blackberries!" exclaimed Mary.

"I thought your exertions should have some reward," rejoined Kate, "and now you may repay yourselves by all the berries you can pick."

"Thank you"—"thank you," they severally replied, profiting by the permission.

"Oh, dear!" exclaimed Lizzy, with pain.

"I forgot," rejoined Kate, "I should have charged the gentlemen first to have plucked the briars from the bushes, that you might gather the fruit without the fear of such dangerous wounds."

"We would rather pluck the berries, and offer them, without the dangers of the thorns, for your acceptance, ladies," answered Mr. Sumpter.

"Not for me," replied Kate. "I prefer the pleasure of gathering them. But where are Dan and Mary? I will seek them, for you know small children may get lost in the woods, and dread the bears."

She was soon out of sight. The colour deepened in Lizzy's cheeks, for Kate's rallery in the morning had made her sensitive.

"Your brother says," remarked Mr. Sumpter, "that Miss Marvin's nature is either wax or ice. One impression either effaces another, or she is too cold and adamantine to receive impressions of friendship and love."

"My brother is ungenerous: besides, he does not understand her. Because she is not an open book, that all may read, he thinks the pages all a blank. A kinder or a warmer heart does not exist in the wide universe, than in the breast of Kate Marvin," earnestly rejoined Lizzy.

The excitement of her feelings at her brother's want of generosity, and the deep truth of her love for Kate, animated her countenance, as she stood with her bonnet thrown back and one hand partly raised in the warmth of her defence. Her small, fairy form seemed to dilate with consciousness of her own truth; and her usually pale and and placid features coloured with indignation towards her brother, while love and tenderness rested in them for Kate.

"She is certainly fortunate in her advocate," continued the gentleman, while a smile of admiration lighted his features. "I certainly would willingly be accucused of much worse than coldness, were I sure of being defended with such warm affection, by one so lovely."

Lizzy's eyes immediately sought the ground.

"Perhaps," said she, wanting to say something, and in confusion from the undisguised admiration of the gentleman—"perhaps, towards your sex she does not feel such ardent friendship as they would be happy to inspire; but I am sure it is not from coldness, or the want of those kindly sympathies which bind one to another."

"Perhaps," he rejoined, "her fortune has been like mine; she never has loved, because she has not found one who pleased both her fancy and her judgment. But I cannot plead this any longer."

Fortunately or unfortunately, Dan and Mary emerged from the bushes but a few paces from them; and interruptions may sometimes be accounted fortunate, and sometimes unfortunate.

"Truants!" exclaimed Lizzy; "but where is Kate?"

"We have not seen her," replied Dan.

"She left us to seek you," rejoined Lizzy.

Kate soon made her appearance, with a basket constructed from leaves pinned together, filled with berries.

"See!" said she, holding up her basket, "the fruits of my ingenuity and industry. But come, good folks; if you have improved the time as I have done, you are ready to return;" and she cast a quizzical look at both the ladies, which called a blush into their cheeks.

John Neal, I think it is, has said, "that there is danger in going a blackberrying with a pretty girl;" and doubtless the Hon. Mr. Sumpter might have said that there was truth in the remark.

The party returned; but Kate was the only one who did not seem to be deeply interested in his or her own thoughts. She saw, but appeared not to notice, their abstraction, only remarking mischievously, when they arrived at the house.

"There, I have brought you all back; but if you had been left to yourselves, I do not believe one of you would have known the way."

"We certainly are much indebted to Miss Marvin," rejoined Mr. Sumpter, "for her safe guidance, as well as keeping off the bears, while we were regaling ourselves with those delicious berries."

Mr. Sumpter soon after returned to his lodgings, where he found his father in a high state of excitement.

The father and son were alike, yet the resemblance was not perfect. Both were tall and of commanding presence, but the heaven-blue eye of the son, which told of benevolence and trust, was not inherited from the sire. The father's eye was of a jet and piercing black, and its restlessness betokened impatience and hasty passions. Both foreheads were intellectual, but the son's seemed the superior, or perhaps it was the more ample development of that portion of the brain, where phrenologists have located benevolence.

The old gentleman was scarce sixty years of age, but his appearance might have well betokened "three-score and ten." Sorrow, or the strength of his passions, or both, had deprived him of the enjoyments of "a green and hale old age."

"Charles," said the old gentleman with agitation, when his son entered his room, "I am sure now I have some traces of them."

"Why so, my dear sir?" replied his son.

"The landlord has been giving me a long account of a woman and her son, who inhabited some hut in these mountains for years. The description of the woman answers for your mother, and the age of the boy for Legrand. Besides, that was the boy's name."

"The similarity of names cannot be relied upon. But does he know anything of them now?"

"No: the boy left here seven or eight years ago, and the mother about four years since. They came, he says, no one knew whence, and they have gone none knows whither. But we will seek them."

"Where will you go?"

"Go! go to the world's end but I will find them. I will wring their secret from that old hypocrite yet."

"Persuasion has heretofore proved unavailing—and force cannot be used."

"But I will use it. He shall tell me where my wife and child are, or else "—but his emotion and rage prevented further utterance.

"All that man can do, I will do for you, my father; but do not, I entreat you, do not let these paroxysms of feeling endanger your life. Command yourself, my dear sir; and now, what shall be our first move?"

"Let us go hence—let us see him again."

Preparations for departure were soon arranged, and before night-fall they were on their way to a distant city.

After issuing his orders for horses, the younger gentleman seized a moment to bid his new friends a hasty and kind adieu. "I sincerely hope," said he, "to meet you all again;" and as he pressed Lizzy's hand in farewell, he added in a low tone of entreaty, "Will you not accompany your father to Washington next winter? Promise me this," and he lowered his head to catch the tones of her voice. "Time admits of no explanation—but will you grant my boon?"

"Yes," she faintly but confidently answered; and they parted in full faith and confidence of each other's affections.

To me, there is something strange in this deep sympathy of soul with soul. It does not require professions, or a long series of acts of kindness to win the confidence of the true-hearted. The gushing feelings of the heart bubble up from their well-fount, until the bosom thrills with its own joyous and delightful emotions.

Are these flowers of love and kindness confined to the favoured few, gifted with more than earthly natures? Or are they the spontaneous production of every heart, until the weeds of selfishness and sin destroy the purity of the soil which alone can give them birth?

When the spirit concentrates within itself, and garners up the store of its tenderness and hopes, and offers them in truth, love and confidence upon any shrine, be it human or divine, the act of sacrifice awakens the deepest and holiest emotions of our nature. It awakens a bliss of joy too deep for mere words to convey the idea of its intensity. A heart divided, cannot receive the reward of its sacrifice. A part may not be accepted. We cannot love the object of our earthly affections, while wealth, station, and the adventitious aids of nature are entangled in the web of our desires. The sacrifice of love, is of soul to soul. Mind and matter cannot mingle and produce the pure essence of its bliss.

And this undivided sacrifice of the heart—this offering in purity and truth, without doubt—whether it be to God, or to an earthly object, calls into exercise the true divinity of our nature, and gives to humanity a glimpse of the enjoyment of Heaven—where all is mind, where all is soul—where truth, love, and confidence exist without alloy.

And although the emotions which it begets are but the result of the natural laws of our being—although the enjoyments which it engenders, are but the prerogative of our nature—yet, as the world is, man has scarcely been wild, when he deemed it " miraculous."

CHAPTER XXI.

THE sudden departure of Mr. Sumpter was a matter of speculation to the circle that his gallantry and intelligence had enlivened. They regretted his absences, but as Lizzy's and Dan's stay was drawing to a close, other circumstances soon engrossed their more particular attention. One was the unexpected arrival of Mr Grant—unexpected to Lizzy and Kate, but the visit had been granted to Dan's solicitations. Uuknown to them, he had progressed much further in his wooing than they had anticipated, and his father had been summoned to attend his nuptials.

Dan's feelings were quiet and reflective, and his tastes strongly domestic. Nothing was more in discordance with his love of quiet, than fashionable amusements, and the glitter of fashionable parade. For a moment he might be startled into admiration by the brilliancy of a comet, but it was the steady light of the fixed stars that fastened his attention, and awoke the deeper feelings of his contemplative nature.

The unobtrusive worth of Mary's character, had won his respect the winter she passed in New-York; and a more intimate acquaintance amid the scenes of her own home, where she felt no restraint from the novelty which surrounded her, had called forth a more ardent estimation of her goodness. Her lameness which she had regarded as an unsurmountable objection to her ever forming a matrimonial alliance, gave her an additional claim upon his tenderness; and, as he averred to her, was but an "additional guarantee that his home would never be desecrated by scenes of fashionable folly and dissipation."

Whether his logic convinced her scruples, or whether her own feelings began to preponderate the balance in his favour, we cannot say. These quiet matches, whether of love or convenience, give not much scope to the historian's pen. But she consented to become his wife, and his father was summoned for his consent and presence at the ceremony.

"Well, Mary," said Kate, "this is arriving at conclusions philosophically, and making the first and last act of the drama at one rising of the curtain."

"But there has been a prologue," rejoined Mary.

"True, but that was rehearsed in the green-room before the play was announced But we will not quarrel about the commencement, so long as we are to witness the finale. But am I to be one of the bridesmaids?"

"Dear Kate, I do dot want any bridesmaid. The contrast between yourself and me on such an occasion would be painful."

"Pshaw," replied Kate; "you will always remember something that everybody else forgets. Why, Mary, I should have loved you as well, could you have been the rival of all my wild sports and mischief. But where is Lizzy—sister Lizzy, dear?"

They sought her, and discovered her in a retired bower in the garden, in conversation with her father. They retreated, and would have retired without speaking; but Lizzy caught a view of them through the interstices of the bower, and called them to join her. The conversation naturally turned upon the approaching wedding.

"Dan and Mary," said Kate, addressing Mr. Grant, "have been so very still about the matter, that I hardly dreamed of your being summoned on their account; but for Lizzy, I can hardly say as much. In truth there seems something like magic in our country air—see the beautiful carnation upon Lizzy's cheeks."

"Are you the only one exempt from its magical influence, Miss Marvin?" rejoined Mr. Grant.

"Oh, cruel!" continued she, "to remind me that neither town nor country is propitious to me. Past twenty-five, and not won or wooed,"

"But you may apply the adage for your consolation," returned Mr. Grant; "As good a fish in the sea as ever was caught."

"Thank you, thank you," rejoined Kate, "for the small portion of comfort its application affords me. Verily I believe, if I ever do marry, I shall have to fish my husband from the vasty deep."

"Yes! you will bait your hook, and then run and leave the line for fear some silly fish may be caught," remarked Dan, who had approached them unperceived.

"A second Daniel—a Daniel come to judgment!" exclaimed Kate, "but it is the deep generosity of my nature to leave the line, that my friends may secure my first bites. Their modesty might have prevented them from ever casting a line. But, good-bye. I promised my good mother to be at her bidding at this hour." And leaving them, she returned to the house.

The conversation between Lizzy and her father, which Mary and Kate had in-

terrupted, had been respecting Mr. Sumpter. That gentleman had called upon Mr. Grant, as he passed through New-York, and with the frankness of a noble mind, actuated by honourable intentions, had informed him of his attachment to his daughter, and his hope that his affections were reciprocated by her. He solicited approbation of his suit, and frankly asked that Lizzy might accompany her father to Washington next winter.

No. 8.

"Between the calls of my country and my duty to my father,'" said he, "I have no time that I can call my own."

The whole matter was as pleasing as unexpected to Mr. Grant, and he cordially gave his assent to the gentleman's solicitations. He received from him a written message to forward to Lizzy, of which he had been the bearer himself.

"There is not a man of my acquaintance," said he, in assuring his daughter of his entire approbation, "whom I should be more proud to call my son-in-law, than Charles Sumpter, of South Carolina."

The appearance of Kate and Mary, as before recorded, interrupted the conversation. After Kate left them, both Lizzy and Mary reproved Dan for the caustic spirit which he ever manifested towards her.

"It is for her good," said he, in extenuation. "At heart she is a downright coquette; but her love of approbation keeps her from any overt act of treachery."

"You are mistaken, brother," rejoined Lizzy; "at heart she is true. But the vivacity of her feelings sometimes carries her so far, that you ascribe it to vanity and love of notoriety."

"I am inclined to think Lizzy right," remarked Mr. Grant. Besides, whatever her feelings might have been towards her foreign admirer, it is evident now, that time has blunted the sorrows of memory, and she only remembers him with the kindly regret of far off circumstances."

"I do not think," said Mary in continuation, "that Kate ever loved Don Sebastian, or would have married him if he had lived. She regretted his death deeply—she said that she had been unjust to him—her deep affection for Donna Maria made her strongly feel for her grief at the loss of her only brother. Besides, her feelings could not have been other than painfully grateful for the magnificent bequest which he had left in token of his regard—but after all this, her feelings toward him were never those of love."

"Mary, you make the case worse," rejoined Dan. "Think you his feelings could have been so deeply interested, if he had found no encouragement from her —no semblance of a return of his affections?"

"It is useless," returned Lizzy, "to try to convince prejudice, but do you think she would love her parents so tenderly, and her female friends so truly, were she the cold and heartless being you deem her?"

And in a pet Lizzy followed Kate to the house. The subject was not continued after she left the garden, for Mary was too submissive and modest to persist in advancing her own convictions. Dan loved her too well to wish to pain her by animadversions upon her friend, and Mr. Grant was not sufficiently intimate with the subject of their remarks, to judge who was in error.

How erroneously we judge of others' motives and feelings! Could the heart be laid bare, and we see its secret cares and sorrows—its incentives to action, and the hidden promptings of the spirit—would there not be more sympathy, more charity, more justice? Only the truly vicious need fear such a scrutiny; and for them, could we know all their temptations, their peculiar weaknesses, perhaps even for them we would feel more forgiveness—more of the spirit to say "Brother go, and sin no more."

The bridal morn at length arrived. It was a beautiful and brilliant day—such an one as the prophets of all ages have hailed as auspicious of the future happiness of those to be wedded. The party was small—none but the particular friends of the family having been invited; for at such an hour, Mary felt that she could not endure the idle gaze of curiosity.

After the company were assembled, and the minister waited to perform the ceremony, Mary entered the room leaning upon the arm of her father, who, as he advanced, rendered her up to the expectant bridegroom. As he did so, his venerable and patriarchal form trembled with the intensity of his emotion. A tear, which could not be repressed, trembled in his eye, and fell upon his time-furrowed cheek. Her mother sobbed audibly, as the clergyman petitioned that the blessings of the Most High might rest upon the union about to be consummated. She was their last, their only child. The other they had consigned to the final resting-place of man. And now, their dear Mary was to be consigned to the care of one dearer than father or mother. Their emotion was contagious; and the deep sympathy of all present was called forth by the solemnity of the scene.

And that a wedding can be ever otherwise than a solemn scene, is a matter of surprise. The union is for life—a partnership, at best of sorrow as well as joy —the sacred and irrevocable vows then uttered by the changing mortals, to know no more change until death. It is but the grace of God and the truth and fervency of their own affections, that may keep them as truly as then promised, and as inviolate as the happiness of the marriage life demands. No doubt, no distrust, no coldness, no indifference should ever be allowed with its breath to sully the mirror of conjugal love. All unkindness and neglect are mortal deformities and death, which should not be deemed possible in domestic union.

After the newly married pair had received the congratulations of their friends they departed, accompanied by Mr. Grant and Lizzy, for their future residence in the city.

CHAPTER XXII.

A FEW weeks subsequently to the events recorded in the close of the last chapter, Kate received a welcome communication from Donna Maria, stating that the marquis had received and accepted the appointment of minister from the court of Spain to the government of the United States, and that they should sail for America soon after the departure of the letter. It closed with a request that she would meet them at New York. She made immediate preparations for compliance, and as it was also probable that she would accompany the marquis's family to Washington, her parents chose to remain in the quiet and comfort of their country home.

As the marquis had not arrived when she reached the city, the interim was devoted to her friends,

"My dear Miss Marvin!" exclaimed Doctor Sprague, the first time he met her after her return; "How refreshing it is to see you again! I declare, the city has been desolate during your absence."

"I cannot comprehend how any spot could be desolate," returned Kate, "where Doctor Sprague claimed an abiding place."

"Your rural summer has not rusted the polish of your compliments," rejoined the doctor. "But will you not take me into the country next summer?"

"Certainly; nothing would give me more pleasure than the presence of Doctor Sprague. But what selfishness is hidden beneath the request?"

"You have given Dan a lily for his attendance. Is there not a rose left for me?"

"There are many left 'to waste their sweetness on the desert air.' But, my dear sir, you surely forget that 'every rose has its thorn?'"

"No matter; some pretty flower for me."

"I have a brilliant *parterre* of poppies and dandelions. To you shall be given the first choice."

"It shall not be the thistle transplanted to our city."

"It is hard for thee to kick against the pricks."

"What! impious as well as saucy?"

"I but quoted the words of truth."

"And truth from you almost becomes doubtful in its import."

"While error from you seems so like truth, that men believe. The difference is in the happy skill of him who can make sophistry seem both reason and argument."

"A war of words, as usual, between wit and wisdom," interrupted Dan.

"Nothing but Mr. Grant's superior penetration would have been able to discover either," rejoined Kate ; "but we know him to be an alchymist, who can turn everything he touches into gold."

"Therefore it cannot be a matter of surprise," continued the doctor ; "that to him the common pebble is as valuable as the most polished diamond."

"I but illustrate the truth, that a third party interfering between two belligerent ones, is doomed to receive the shots of both," returned Dan.

"But the bulletin report will be 'wounded, but not killed,' " remarked Kate. "Remember, doctor, that my prettiest dandelion is yours," and she moved to the other side of the room.

"Who is that gentleman who just entered?" she inquired of Aunt Martha.

"Mr. Thompson. Your memory surely must be poor, to have forgotten so ardent an admirer," replied Aunt Martha.

"I recognised his countenance, but his name had escaped me," continued Kate ; "but I thought Mr. Thompson was in the 'far west.' I have not seen him since my first winter in New York."

"For four or five years past he has been gathering fame and wealth in Ohio ; but he is now upon a visit, and also, report says, to find a wife. So have your cap in its prettiest fix," rejoined Aunt Martha.

"Oh, dear! its strings are—" but her lamentation was cut short by the approach of the gentleman they were canvassing. "He is homely enough," thought Kate; "to be a member of Congress."

And truly, as far as beauty was concerned, he might have claimed a seat in that honourable body. Embrowned by the exposure of his journey, tall and sinewy, long-favoured, with large mouth, eyes and nose ; and to add to his graces, his hair was brushed, after the fashion of the day, in a perpendicular position from his forehead. Nothing but bristles could have stood so straight, without the aid of a barber's genius. His forehead was ample and bold, and he might have been forgiven for exposing the only feature that could claim any pretensions to beauty ; but its height only made his face longer, and the addition was anything but favourable to the general contour.

His dress was strictly in fashion ; but the fashion was anything but adapted to him. A long blue coat, which might have originated the hint of "Jim Crow's long-tailed blue ;" a buff vest, and very light-coloured pants, full and flowing like a Turk's trowsers. The *tout ensemble* was almost ludicrous. And besides, it looked so new, and so strictly the fashion, that one well acquainted with the little details which make a gentleman's dress, without looking so finished—so strictly from the tailor's and barber's hands, could hardly but think that an ourang-outang had been caught, and fitted out with the fixtures of a gentleman.

He also appeared ill at ease in his new coat, and consequently embarrassed in his manner.

As he passed along and was recognised, the mothers received him very graciously, but the daughters scarcely noticed him, except with a stare. When he reached Aunt Martha and Kate, he courteously saluted the former ; and then, as if half doubting the propriety of the act, turned to the latter.

"Miss Marvin, I believe," said he, hesitatingly.

"Yes," she replied, frankly extending her hand, with one of her most gracious smiles ; "and I am truly unfortunate if I have lost my identity in Mr. Thompson's memory."

"Not lost—not lost," he replied with animation ; "but I feared that another name, ere this, might have been your right and title."

"An unfortunate allusion, my dear sir, to remind a lady that she is not married, but approaching a 'certain age.' But," she added, before he could express any gallant parry to her remark ; "I believe you are recently from the west—that land of imagination and brave hearts. I am going to be selfish, and claim you all my own, until you have given me a description of the country, the inhabitants, society there, and everything." And she moved, so that he could have a place beside her.

Her frank cordiality of manner relieved his embarrassment, and he seated himself, with a gratified look for her kindness.

His intelligent descriptions of western scenes and character, and the animated vivacity with which he portrayed his sketches, combined with his piquant comparisons of frontier and genteel society, soon proved that, if his graces had somewhat rusted, his knowledge of "men and things" amply made up for the deficiency.

Doctor Sprague soon joined them, and a group gathered around, and in listening to the animated and interesting conversation maintained between the gentlemen, forgot to trifle.

"We are indebted to Mr. Thompson for our evening's entertainment," said Kate to Doctor Sprague, as the company broke up; "a sensible man has for once compelled a fashionable party to act like rational beings."

The alluring beauty of the autumnal sky the next morning, drew forth a party for a country excursion. The arrangements were speedily made, and about half-past eight o'clock in the morning, they embarked in a small steam-boat, which had been chartered for their accommodation, and proceeded up the North River. After about three hours' sail, they landed at one of those pleasant villages, which, from the days of Diedrich Knickerbocker, have graced the beautiful valley of the Hudson.

All the carriages of the place were called into requisition, to convey the party inland; but of the shapeable ones, there were not enough to convey a moiety of the ladies. The gentlemen had provided for themselves such as they could get; and hay-carts and lumber-waggons, besides divers nameless Dutch inventions of locomotion, were among the number. According to right and etiquette, the married ladies were first served with the most desirable means of conveyance; and then the other ladies, as best might be.

Kate and Lizzy, supported by Aunt Martha, refused to be seated until they should see all the other ladies provided for; and the result was, that a hay-cart was the most desirable vehicle left. "This is as it should be," observed Kate with a laugh, when they were seated; "a rural excursion should have a rural carriage for conveyance. Our party is just right. Mr. Thompson for charioteer, and Mr. Grant and Doctor Sprague for attendants. Commerce, law, and philosophy."

"Accompanied by wit, beauty, and truth," gallantly interrupted the doctor.

"Oh, if Dan and Mary were only here!" remarked Lizzy.

"Let them alone," returned the doctor; "they are enjoying the 'sweets of matrimony—'"

"Shut up in a close carriage, and even denied the free air of the country," interrupted Aunt Martha.

"But to the single of all ages," continued the doctor, "it is allowed to enjoy individual freedom and—"

"A pleasant ride in a hay-cart," quickly added Kate.

And the pleasures of that ride were long after remembered and referred to.

After proceeding four or five miles inland, they reached a beautiful upland grove of chestnut and walnut trees. Their pioneers immediately halted, and permission from the owner was procured by a tangible consideration, while the party alighted. The wants of appetite had not been forgotten by the more considerate of the party; and bread, cheese, dried beef, and so forth, were brought from some of the wagons in abundance.

"Our fare," remarked Doctor Sprague, "may not be of such a quality as some of our ladies may think the most palatable; but open air, exercise, and a little fatigue, are the best seasoning for any dish, and I trust we shall not have to carry any one back defunct from starvation. Our dessert may be found upon the tres, and under them."

Truth compels us to add, that however delicate a fashionable lady's appetite may be at home on ordinary occasions, there was no one present at that time but who did ample justice to the food provided.

After they had dined, in penetrating the grove farther Kate discovered a fine large stump. "A rostrum," she exclamed, "for a stump orator—where is Mr. Thompson?"

"Mr. Thompson! a stump speech from Mr. Thompson!" loudly reiterated Doctor Sprague.

The call collected the wanderers around the spot, and to promote the hilarity of the scene, Mr. Thompson, without demur, ascended the stump.

"Ladies and gentlemen," said he; "one of the fundamental principles of enjoyment in a scene like this is, that each and every one yield whatever may be in his or her power, to the sum of general amusement. Here, as in every body politic the general welfare provides for individual happiness. And although this is your first rural party, it may not be your last; therefore, pardon me, for offering a few suggestions which may add a second time to the amount of your pleasure.

"The first thing to be considered is that you must resolve to be pleased with your pleasures, and amused with your amusements. There necessarily will be some little annoyances; but if they are met with a spirit of accommodation and good-nature, they will cease to annoy, and only become sources of happiness.

" An instance of the kind has occurred to-day. Some of the ladies here present were obliged to accept seats in a hay-cart. Instead of being annoyed by the uncouthness of their carriage, they were pleased to consider it most in keeping with the object of the party, and therefore, the most desirable. And by their vivacity and good-nature, they rendered a ride in a hay-cart an event more pleasing, more worthy to be remembered, than one could have been in the most splendid barouche that ever rolled upon wheels, with less amiable and pleasant society.

"Another very important item in your comfort will be, to leave everything at home that you fear of soiling. In matters of dress, this rule must be self-evident. But it is also necessary in many little peculiarities of character. If your pride is annoyed by excusable familiarity, or your sensitiveness wounded by many nameless grievances that may occur, roll them up safely with everything of a like nature, and leave them in some safe deposit at home. It will add to your own, as well as to the general happiness.

"Another consideration. Let each one endeavour to keep his neighbour in countenance, should aught occur to mar his enjoyment. I remember a happy illustration of this spirit that I witnessed a few months since, at a party of a similar character in the west. In crossing a ditch, one of the young ladies slipped and soiled her dress. The accident annoyed her; and others gathered around, some to condole, and others to try to remedy the misfortune. The latter was impossible, as the water was muddy. At that moment the sprightly daughter of a noble Kentuckian, whom our whole country delights to honour, came up, and upon being informed of the nature of the mishap, 'Shades,' said she 'give the finishing touch to the picture, and I cannot allow one to monopolize the whole!' and in an instant her own spotless robe was as soiled as the other. 'We,' she added, with her own merry inimitable grace, 'belong to the brave duck tribe, who delight in mud-puddles.' And putting her arm through the lady's immediately walked on. I need not add, that any accident of a similar nature that day was not a source of discomfort.

"And lastly, start prepared. If the sun shines, it may not be amiss to take an umbrella; and remember what you must have, and leave everything that may be a source of care. I have answered the call, and now resign the stump to my honourable colleague, Doctor Sprague."

Thus called upon, the doctor could not refuse; and mounting the stump with a ludicrously wry face, "My honourable friend," said he, "has scarcely left anything for me to say, but that I heartily concur in his bill of instructions. I will only add, that should any of you ever attend a rural party in the winter, it will add much to your enjoyment to take skates and snow-shoes."

A laugh rewarded his forethought and eloquence, and the party, delighted with everything, prepared for their return.

How little it requires to make us happy, when we are disposed to be so !

A cloudless sky and a brilliant moon, made their return on the river not the least delightful portion of the day's enjoyment ! and they arrived in New York between nine and ten in the evening, as tired and happy as an exhilarating day of innocent and cheerful amusement could make them.

———————

CHAPTER XXIII.

THE arrival of the marquis interrupted Kate's further participation in the convivial circles of her friends in New York ; and his official duties requiring his presence at Washington, thither he immediately repaired, accompanied by his family and Kate.

Her meeting with Donna Maria was saddened by retrospection ; but Donna Maria had been so wont to associate her memory with the sound of a merry laugh and gay sallies of wit, that she strove to bury her own regrets, and provoke the lively tone of former days.

Little Don Carlos, now a fine lad, oftener than aught else brought back the vivid remembrance of Don Sebastian to the minds of both. In features, he was the picture of his uncle ; and, in addition, he possessed much of Don Sebastian's natural vivacity and high-toned feeling.

He was a bold, courageous and spirited boy ; and both of his parents, when they noted his resemblance, in feature and character, to him now no more, ardently prayed that his life might be more worthily spent, and not so tragically ended. His father had taken him from the convent where he had been placed for his education, as his mother would not consent to a separation of distance ; and on their arrival at Washington, he was entered as a border in one of the Catholic schools at Georgetown.

Although it was too early for the fashionable season to commence, the families of some of the members of Congress had already arrived, and the appearance of other distinguished individuals soon began to give an earnest of brilliant circles that a winter in Washington ever creates.

In Washington there is perhaps more independence of particular fashions—less observation of the precise detail of conventional rules, than in any other American city. The leading *ton* are already distinguished, and do not fear the accidental collision of " little great folks." The peculiar position of the politicians compels them to notice with something of attention the hangers-on of their party—on whom, perhaps, they are unable to bestow more desirable acts of consideration.

Concentrating, as the winter population there does, from the wide separated sections of our common country, they meet more upon the basis of equality, than elsewhere. An introduction to some one of the many distinguished personages there, and lodgings at Gadsby's are the only *prima facie* evidences required of character and worth.

" A winter in Washington ?" How incongruous are thousands of its recollections ! And we will venture to assert, that to one unconnected with party politics—to one who is not seeking either office or emolument ; and to those to whom the smiles and promises of great men are matters of indifference—no place presents more attractive scenes of enjoyment. There is always some new motion in the House—some belligerent move among its members, some duel, or some other exciting topic, which creates an interest in all the different grades, and keeps the life-pool from stagnating.

A few days before the House convened, Mr. Grant and Lizzy made their appearance. Mr. Sumpter had arrived before them, and ignorant of Kate's presence there, they met the next morning at Mr. Grant's lodgings. He was dressed in mourning, and upon his countenance was impressed the bereavement of his heart. His father was dead. He merely communicated the event, stating that it occurred on his way south, while in Philadelphia.

But upon his own mind was stamped, in characters of anguish, that his father was the victim of his own ungovernable passions. To these had been sacrificed the happiness of his manhood; his remorse had brought on premature old age; and finally, his life paid the forfeit of his faults and crimes.

" Crimes," may be a strong term to use in connection with the name of a man, who stood before the world with spotless integrity and most honourable fame. But are cruelty and injustice, although they may be the result of a moment of passion, less than crime? Is he excusable, who will allow one act of unexplained mystery to outweigh a life of unsuspected virtue and affection? And can it be less than criminal for a man, for any cause, to inflict a blow upon the wife of his bosom?

The father of Charles Sumpter had married, early in life, a young and lovely orphan of French descent. She was a lively, graceful child of nature, ardent in her feelings and temperament, but guided by impulse rather than by any fixed principle of right. The alliance had been of love, without any consideration of interest. But he was justified in his choice; for if she brought him not much wealth, his own coffers were overflowing, and she possessed beauty, grace, accomplishments, an affectionate disposition, and a brilliant imagination. She was all he asked, and the first years of their wedded life were replete with the happiness which he desired.

But she had one fault; she loved mystery. Whether it was an innate quality of her mind, or had been imbibed from the romances of her native tongue, it mattered not. But it hung like a cloud over her better faculties, and mystifying everything that she exerted herself about, she enveloped herself in the haze of her own fancyings.

This was his only source of inquietude, and it seriously annoyed him—for his nature was as frank and open as the broad scroll of nature. Both were passionate, but his was the most forgiving temper. He was easily ruffled, and as easily appeased, while his passions were seldom aroused to the depths of their own own strength; but when once awakened, they were cruelly unforgiving.

Perhaps, had she been guided, her fault might have been corrected; but she never knew reproof—no one counselled her. Her husband often reproached her, but that she regarded as the ebullition of his spleen, and his fault instead of her own.

They had been married about eight years, and their second child was about four years old, when, during his wife's absence from home, he accidentally examined a secret drawer in her *escritoire*, and discovered some letters, which breathed the most ardent love and gratitude to the lady to whom they were addressed. The signature was only initials, and the superscription was to his wife. The date was some five years previously, and the handwriting was evidently too bold and manly for a female correspondent and friend.

Aware that his wife stood isolated in the world, save in connection with himself, a passionate jealousy took possession of his breast, and he tortured both his imagination and memory to elucidate the mystery. He could only remember, that at some time a few years previously, his wife had visited an acquaintance in Virginia: and instantly it flashed upon his mind, that the writer was some more than proper acquaintance formed during that visit. Well would it have been for him if idleness (for it was not curiosity) had not prompted him to investigate the contents of his wife's desk.

Never until then had the most remote thought sullied his wife's fidelity—not a doubt had questioned her entire and devoted regard to him. But now his whole fabric of happiness was blasted by the first suspicion. Let jealousy and doubt have but one item to work upon, and soon they will raise a hydra monster as hideous as their own deformity.

He called his little son to him, and in each feature traced some dissimilarity to his own. The child had been thought the picture of his father, save that he had inherited a delicacy of constitution from his mother and the circumstances of his birth, which had been premature.

He awaited his wife's return with the feelings of a demon, rather than those of a man. That he had been duped without a suspicion, added tenfold to his vindictiveness. He examined nothing—he sought nothing, but the confirmation of his horrid doubts.

When she arrived, he met her with the stoical calmness of a martyr; and having conducted her to their private dressing-room, immediately, and without a

No. 9.

word, retired. She was a little surprised at his manner, but busy in disrobing herself, she thought no more of it ; and when she had flung aside her mantle and bonnet, threw herself upon a pile of cushions, which were placed in the recess of a window.

It was not long before her husband returned, leading by the hand her youngest and therefore her favourite child. She sprang from her couch with a mother's delight to greet her little boy, but her husband's hand put her back, and in a stern and unnatural voice he asked,—

" Woman, whose child is this ?"

She looked at him bewildered by the interrogatory.

" Ah, I wonder not that you are confounded and speechless," he continued :— " Be assured that I know all your perfidy and baseness! Extenuation or forgiveness is impossible—go ; and take the offspring of a guilty amour with you—from this hour you are a stranger in my house, or memory. But I will not send you off as destitute as I took you—in your maiden name, at my banker's, you will find funds deposited. But to-morrow morning, let me not find you in this house !" and he turned to leave the room.

Amazement had prevented her from interrupting him; but as he was closing the door, she started from her stupor.

" Charles !" she exclaimed, " are you mad ? What do you mean ?"

" Mean ? I mean that I am no longer ignorant of your guilt."

" Guilt? of what have I been accused ?"

" It needs no name—but go, lest I forget you are a woman, and fell you to the floor ?"

" It would be less cruel than the taunts of your wild frenzy."

" And who has been the cause of my frenzy, base woman?"

" Base woman !" she replied, her indignation wholly mastering the stupor of her amazement, " and who dares call me base, save my own husband ?"

" And what is that but the offspring of your guilt and crime ?" rejoined he, spurning with his foot the child.

This aroused the very depth of her passions. She had been accused herself of what she knew not—but to see her child spurned by the author of its being—it was more than woman could bear, and she turned with bitter fury in her words and manner. This enraged him the more, until in his ungovernable fury at her imagined duplicity and resentment, he struck her. She staggered beneath the blow, but did not fall, and recovering herself, she turned with a frightful calmness towards him.

" I go," said she, " but think not that I will accept any of your bounty—no although we should perish,' and she clasped her little boy with frantic wildness to her breast, " I would not taste a mouthful of food that your money purchased. There was a legacy of five thousand dollars left me by my aunt; give me that, and a knowledge of your cruelly treated wife and injured child shall trouble you no more."

" My child !" said he, with bitterness : " but take what you will; there is thrice the amount of that paltry legacy already deposited in your name at my banker's."

" But think not," said she again, arresting his footsteps as he turned to leave the apartment, " that our wrongs and our crimes will go unpunished. Remorse, when it is too late, shall torture you, till the grave hides you from the sight of man. Your death-bed shall be desolate." But the thought of her other child arrested her curse or prophecy, and in a softened tone, with the anxiety of a mother's undefined dread resting in her voice, she continued,—

" But where is Charles? he goes with me, too."

" You will see him no more—I have sent him away."

" Fiend !" but he was gone, and she remained alone in her bitterness.

In the morning she was gone ; and from that time all trace of her disappeared. He inquired at his banker's, and found that the sum of the legacy had been drawn, but nothing more. Not doubting that she had gone to the partner of her guilt, he desired no information of her continued existence.

Without any explanation to his friends, in answer to their inquiries for his wife, he desired her name might never be mentioned to him. To put off little Charles, who was incessant in his pleadings for his "dear mamma," was a harder task. The child would not forget the dearest object of his affections. And to drive the remembrance of his mother from his mind, and to escape his maddening inquiries, he was sent to a distant school, that new scenes and thoughts might banish her recollection.

Time progressed. Charles arrived at manhood, and amid the busy scenes of active life, the memories of his childhood were as far-off dreams. His father, in the thought that he was a wronged man, justified himself for his harshness.

Four years previously to their northern tour, which introduced them within the precincts of our narrative, a gentleman called upon Mr. Sumpter, and after remarking that he had but recently returned from the East Indies, inquired for Mrs. Sumpter, a lady, he added, to whom he owed great obligations and everlasting gratitude.

"There must be some mistake," quickly returned Mr. Sumpter; "I have no wife. Besides, of your name or countenance I have not the most distant recollection."

"To you, sir," rejoined the gentleman, "I am a stranger. But tell me, is my noble benefactress dead?"

"I know not to whom you refer," answered Mr. Sumpter.

"I refer to the lady who was the wife of Mr. Charles Sumpter of this city, twenty—and more than that—twenty-five years ago. How time has passed! I had hoped my kind benefactress would have been spared to receive the acknowledgment of my obligations. But her death does not absolve my honour, any more than it can obliterate my gratitude. My business remains with you."

And he went on to detail, that he met Mrs. Sumpter while she was on a visit to some friends in Virginia, at whose house he was confined both by sickness and want. He was a native of New-England, and had gone south to seek his fortune. During Mrs. Sumpter's stay there, he had received a letter from his friends at the north, stating, that if he could return with a specified sum of money, there was an opportunity for investment in an East India cargo, which would, without doubt, yield a very large return. The information he made a source of actual unhappiness. Nothing but misfortune and sickness had attended him at the south—he was penniless, and but a pensioner upon the bounty of a hospitable Virginian. His irritation of mind brought on a relapse of his fever.

Mrs. Sumpter learned the history of his misfortunes from her friend ; and with the ministering kindness of an angel, sought him, and won from his own lips the tale of his anxieties.

"Is that all?" said she ; "I have more than that sum by me, which my husband gave me to purchase a new set of jewels. I would rather invest it in a venture for a fortune for my little boy," looking at her little son, whom she held by the hand. "Then hurry, and get well, and you shall be my factor—I will furnish the money, and you shall do the business, and give me one-third of the profits. But mind," she added, with a smile, "as it is for Charles, it will be a long while before he will be a man, and I shall insist that you shall keep it in trust and use until then."

Disappointment and anxiety had caused his illness, and hope soon cured it. A variety of circumstances had combined to keep him much of the time from his native land. But the noble lady's venture had been cast by benevolence upon the waters of truth. And now, "after many days," it was to be returned "with usury."

Mr. Sumpter listened to the narration without interruption, and then rising with an air of bewilderment, he left the room. A few minutes elapsed, and he returned, bearing in his hand the ill-fated letters that had murdered his happiness.

"Were you," said he, presenting them to the stranger, "the author of these?"

"Yes," he replied, as he glanced at them. "One I wrote when I first arrived at home, and the other when I embarked on my first voyage. As I never received any acknowledgment of them, I supposed Mrs. Sumpter wanted no further trouble about the matter until I could bring her son a fortune, and I did not write after, even when I was in America; and it is seven years since I have been at home before. But I wait," he added, noticing Mr. Sumpter's abstraction, "to give you the necessary vouchers of your property."

"Go, go," he exclaimed wildly; "I do not want it. You can transact the business with my son," he added, recollecting himself, and ringing the bell, a negro appeared.

"Cato," he continued, "show this gentleman to your master, Charles."

The gentleman withdrew, rightly attributing his abrupt dismissal and Mr. Sumpter's incoherent manner, to his awakened grief for the loss of his amiable lady.

The young gentleman received him cautiously, and with apparent composure listened to the detail of the business. The stranger frankly offered the one-half of his fortune, saying that it was ample, and that he owed the whole to his generous benefactress. His proposition was declined by the young man, and he added, that the tale seemed more like a fairy venture, and the wealth the gift of generous genii, rather than the transaction of a mere money matter of earth. One-third was what his mother had stipulated for, and one-third was all that he would receive.

"Yes," replied the stranger, referring to his former remark, "your mother was the golden fairy of my fortunes. I had always hoped to return to her own hand the money, which she undoubtedly considered but a gift, adding the rest to save the sensitiveness of my feelings. But it has ever been the aim of my life to render her gift a profitable venture to her. But how long," he added, "since she died?"

"I hardly remember my mother," returned the young man, evasively.

"Poor woman!" rejoined the stranger, "she was too good for this world." And he continued the calculation of the table of figures before him, like a man who had spent his life in counting dollars and cents.

After the stranger retired, Charles leaned his head upon his hand, and remained in painful thought. He knew it was not death that had separated his father and mother; but of the true detail of the circumstances which had caused their separation, he was ignorant. After an hour of painful reflection he sought his father.

"Charles," exclaimed the old gentleman, wildly, "I am a murderer. You are dumb. But can my crime be less than that?"

And he proceeded, with vehemence and minute distinctness, to detail every circumstance of finding the letters, and his last unhappy interview with his wife. The ghost of the wrongs he had committed rose vividly before his imagination, and the keen barb of remorse rankled in his inmost soul. His grief at times partook of the nature of a madman. His son used every argument in his power to sooth his frenzy—but who can relieve the anguish of an accusing conscience!

The inquiries which he instituted to discover, if possible, the fate of the fugitives, were as fallacious as he feared they might prove. A quarter of a century is a long time for the clouds of injustice and doubt to thicken over the sun of affection. They had condensed to impenetrable darkness.

Accident revealed to him the name and residence of the executor of his mother's legacy, and he immediately wrote to the gentleman, inquiring for his mother by her maiden name, and desiring to be informed if, at any time within the last twenty-five years, he had known of the residence of the lady inquired for. Some time elapsed before he received a reply, and when it did arrive, it but added to his anguish.

It briefly stated that the lady in question was living, and that the writer had communicated to her the contents of the letter which he had received. And in answer he was instructed to say, that she lived, but to know more of her was impossible: that injustice and cruel wrong had driven her forth desolate, and deserted by every human being upon earth save her youngest child: that reparation for her injuries after so long a period had elapsed, was impossible. It added, that as the inquirer might be her first-born son, her residence should be revealed to him in due time.

As his father was continually accusing himself of being the murderer of his wife and child, Charles communicated to him the contents of the letter. Instead of allaying, it but added oil to the fire of his frenzy. He insisted upon seeing the gentleman who had answered his son's inquiries, and they started for the northern city where he resided.

But persuasion and entreaty were alike fruitless. Nothing was added to the information already given, and they continued their tour still farther north.

The circumstances and causes which led them to retrace their steps, have been already detailed. The father's strength but lasted to reach Philadelphia, where he expired in the arms of his son. In his last moments, he enjoined it upon Charles to seek his mother and brother, and by his care and love for them to teach them to forgive the memory of him who had wronged them. He would have added more, but the death rattle in his throat choked his utterance. He essayed to speak again, but his son could catch merely the sound of the faint murmuring. With the last respiration of nature, he heard the faint murmur of the word, " forgive."

Charles caused the body to be placed in an air-tight coffin, and embarked with it on board a packet for South Carolina. His grief for the death of his father was deep and sincere; and although he could not extenuate the past, yet he felt that the repentance and grief which followed a knowledge of his wrongs, should have met with forgiveness.

His heart yearned for the sympathy of his brother, but his feelings were reluctant to met his mother, and he delayed to claim the knowledge which, on the death of his father, had been promised him.

Those events combined, had kept him from communicating with Lizzy after he had left New-York. And it was with the chastened and subdued feelings of a mourner, that he met her when she arrived in Washington.

CHAPTER XXIV.

The considerate attention, both of the marquis, who had been informed of the young man's bereavement, and Mr. Grant, combined with the gentle tenderness of Lizzy and the cheerful society of Donna Maria and Kate, won him, as spring appeared, to something to his former gay courtesy.

As yet, he shrunk from communicating, even to Lizzy, the history of his parent's transgression. His parents! his clear judgment could see the mutual wrong of both. He had no wish to blame either; and he could forgive, and appreciate the exculpation of each party.

From tenderness to him, Lizzy had not mingled in all the gay scenes of the metropolis; but had she, as usual, been the shadow of her friend, her quick perception would have noted in Kate's manner, on more than one occasion, an embarrassment and silence not in keeping with her usual gay frankness.

There are memories in the heart of every one, which are shielded with the utmost jealousy from every observer. Sometimes in their private hours, Lizzy had noticed a thoughtful abstraction in Kate's manner, and when she railed her upon it, she would reply with a laugh—

" Thoughtful! why, I am approaching a thoughtful age. Past twenty-five and not married. Mary is gone and you are going—is not my approaching loneliness enough to make even me sad? Not a beau left!'

" You forget the venerable Doctor Sprague," rejoned Lizzy.

"I beg his pardon for the omission of my memory—but I surely shall be an old maid, past hope, before he will concentrate the diffusive rays of his affections upon one object."

"Well, you run away from Mr. Thompson—"

"Oh, I never should have courage to ask him—he is so tall—and I am equally sure he never will ask me."

"Kate, in sober earnest, I believe you love your own independence too well to get married."

"I believe independence is a quality not much admired by the gentlemen—"

"Not that—I mean, I do not believe that any offer would tempt you to marry."

"Nevertheless, my whole life has been a search for a husband. To be sure, I have not made it the ostensible object of living, for thst is a matter my good mamma taught me, when a little girl, that I must not tell. She said, that to appear anxious for a husband was a sure scare-crow for the beaux."

The entrance of a servant with a note interrupted her. Lizzy took it, and glancing at its superscription handed it to Kate.

"Here," said she, "is one of your missives from some devoted swain."

Kate broke the seal, and her face became pale as marble, as she glanced at its contents. She hurriedly looked at her watch, and started from her chair.

"Where is your father?" she asked of Lizzy.

"In the house—but what is the matter?"

"Nothing: send for him, while I send for the marquis's carriage; get your bonnet, and we will take an airing in the country—how my head aches."

"Kate, what is the matter? I never saw you look so in my life."

"I have said my head ached—will you send for your father? He must be our beau in a ride."

"Why not send for Charles, if a gentleman's attendance is indispensable?"

"He is gone!"

"Where? why should I not know it?" asked Lizzy in alarm.

"I don't know where—in the country, on a shooting excursion I believe. But here is your father and the carriage too. Come, Mr. Grant," said she, as they met him in the hall, "pray leave the nation to take care of itself this afternoon and go with us."

"Is this for what I was summoned in such haste?" he asked, with almost vexation.

"Certainly," replied Kate, with her usual tone of saucy indifference; "what could be of more consequence than the care of two such amiable and pleasant ladies, as Mr. Thompson was pleased to call us."

"I should have chosen, that you would have selected some younger man for your foolery. My presence is a matter of importance in the house this after-upon. The report of the committee on—"

"Scold me, if you will, when we return; but you must go with us now." Her firm manner and tremulous voice prevented further remonstrance, and he followed her to the carriage.

She gave her directions to the servant in a low tone, and he drove with a rapid pace to the city. The note which Kate had received, ran thus,—

"Catherine Marvin, by the hopes of your own youthful years—by your love of truth—by your desires for our future happiness—delay, interrupt, or prevent, as you best can, the termination of an affair of honour between Legrand de Forest and Charles Sumpter, until half-past six. The meeting is arranged to take place in the meadow of Col. Burton's plantation, at five o'clock this afternoon. Be discreet, and do not betray them to the public authorities, until after the hour I have named. Haste. Legrand now leaving his room."

"THE MOUNTAIN WOMAN."

It was a quarter-past four, when she received the note. Mr. Grant's presence and counsel she first thought necessary, but before his arrival, the dread of a hoax made her afraid to communicate the contents of the note. But who could be the author of such a cruel hoax? who knew, save the marquis and Donna Maria, that she ever saw Legrand de Forest? Not even Lizzy ever heard her mention his name. Who knew of his connection with the Mountain Woman? These, and a thousand other questions, presented themselves. But before they arrived at the meadow designated, she had collected her thoughts, and definitely arranged in her mind how to proceed. She was as calm as when she had stood with a lighted torch over the train of powder, which was to insure her destruction or salvation. Kate Marvin had more strength of nerve than men or women usually possess. She dared, at any time, to execute the promptings of her will—whether of stern resolve, or a matter of mirth.

When they arrived in sight of the meadow, her pulse quickened as she saw two parties entering the grounds from opposite directions. The carriage stopped, and the driver asked further orders. She motioned him to let down the steps, and leaping from the carriage was followed mechanically by Mr. Grant and Lizzy. Their ride had been a silent one, and her companions could not avoid wondering when the new whim of silence was to end.

" Whither are we going?" asked Lizzy in amazement.

" Shooting ducks and catching pigeons," was Kate's ready reply.

" And have you brought me out here for this folly?" asked Mr. Grant, with severe displeasure in his manner.

" My object in bringing you here I have not explained," responded Kate. " I stipulated for no reproof until our return; and then, if you think I merit your displeasure, I will hear all that you may say."

" Is not that Charles?" asked Lizzy, as the keen eye of affection detected his form in the meadow.

" Very likely," replied Kate; " you know I told you he was out on a shooting excursion. Let us join them."

The emphasis of Kate's reply, and the appearance of the parties in the meadow, at once explained to Mr. Grant's comprehension the true position of matters. As he assisted her over the hedge, he pressed her hand, as an intimation that he understood. She replied with an intelligent glance, and hurried directly to the spot which the belligerent parties occupied.

Mr. Grant remembered now, that in the morning he had heard something of a hasty dispute, and high words having passed between Sumpter and an officer in the navy.

The combatants stood with folded arms some paces apart, while the seconds were engaged in arranging the preliminaries; and neither of the parties noticed the approach of a third one, and one so little desired, until Kate, when within a few paces cried out—

" Ha! truant," addressing Sumpter; " I heard that you were out on a snipe shooting excursion, and have come to witness the sport."

He turned, and seeing Kate and her companions, was transfixed.

" Miss Marvin!" he stammered in amazement.

" Have you no other word of welcome?" she returned. " Here, perhaps, to this lady you can say something more interesting than—Miss Grant."

" Why are you here?" he asked in a tone of bitterness, fearing that their appearance might be construed detrimental to his honour.

" Do not fear for our safety. There is no danger that any one will mistake Lizzy for a snipe. There she is, so trembling that I should sooner think her a partridge. But I see you are not my only acquaintance present;" and she approached De Forest.

" Captain de Forest," said she, " I had not thought that when we met again, you would stand aloof with folded arms and moody brow;" and she extended her hand.

" Miss Marvin, I had not thought to meet you here," he replied, slightly touching the hand that she proffered.

" Well, now that you have met me," she rejoined, " you may as well get down off your stilts. I am in no mood to pay much respect to the representative of the god of war. Come; you are not acquainted with my friend, Miss Grant."

"Miss Marvin," he replied, stiffly bowing, "excuse me; I am not in a mood for ladies' society."

"By my truth, De Forest, you must have been to a new school in your study of the tactics of gallantry, since last we met. But will you not introduce me to the gentleman of your party who stands opposite."

"Miss Marvin, I must be excused," he replied, without any relaxation of his cold formality.

"Sir," she responded as haughtily as himself, "I am not wont to be treated so cavalierly. But," she added, again assuming a gay tone, "I came not here to entreat; I am in search of amusement, sport, frolic, or what you will, and I must have your assistance."

"Miss Marvin, I must be excused."

"Where did you learn that parrot phrase? Is it in the rules and regulations of the navy?"

When Kate had left Sumpter, Lizzy put her arm within his, as if for safety from, she knew not what. "Charles," said she, "what does all this mean? Kate acts as though she was crazy—at one moment silent and serious—the next as gay as at a masquerade. Papa is vexed, irritated or pained—and you look so pale and your voice sounds so unnatural."

"Do not ask me now, dearest—to-morrow I will not have a thought that you may not share."

"But now—but now—I cannot wait with this suspense till morning." And a tear glistened on her eyelashes.

He felt that he must be stern—though it rived him to the heart—his honour, his manhood demanded immediate action. The alliance of tenderness would unnerve his hand and purpose. What a paradox is honour!

"Gentlemen," said he to the seconds, who stood apart, "the unexpected presence of these ladies has interrupted our deliberations. With Captain de Forest's concurrence, we will retire to some other place."

His second approached De Forest, and repeated the suggestion of Sumpter. He assented, and bowing to Kate, "Adieu, Miss Marvin—I trust you will be able to find more desirable assistance for your sport, than I should be able to tender—farewell."

And he turned on his heel to follow the gentlemen, who had already started.

"Not so, most gallant captain," returned Kate; "where you go, I go also." And she took hold of his arm, as though her company was a matter of choice, instead of compulsion.

When Sumpter saw De Forest bow to Kate, he turned to Mr. Grant, who had not greeted any of the company, save by a slight nod.

"My dear sir," said Sumpter, "I must resign your daughter to your care;" and he released his arm from Lizzy's.

"If I take her now," replied Mr. Grant coldly, "never with my consent shall she rest again on you for protection."

"Sir!" exclaimed Sumpter in amazement. Lizzy clung tight to his arm in her terror. But they were involuntarily recalled from their painful position by a merry laugh from Kate. It jarred upon their feelings, and they all turned to see why any one could laugh then.

Kate, although her manner bespoke idle folly, and her tone was one of banter, had watched with eagle eye every movement of the different parties. She had noticed the pistols returned to the case and given in charge to the attendant, who was a negro of Sumpter's.

"Captain de Forest," said she, "I will not trouble you more; but the next time we meet, if it is after a six years' absence, I hope you will be in better humour."

"And you less troublesome," he thought, but he merely bowed to her adieu, and walked immediately forward. Quick as thought she turned to Cato, and snatched the case from his hand, saying as she did so, "Fellow, on your life follow me not;" and with the laugh which had arrested their attention, and a merry bound, like a mischievous child, darted towards the river which skirted the meadow.

De Forest had turned at the same sound, and both he and Sumpter, at the same moment, saw the mischief she intended, and started in pursuit. Kate had the

advantage of their moment of surprise and excitement, and which added to the fleetness of her speed. She gained the bank; and with a shout of triumph, for an instant poised the case in the air, and then hurled it with the whole of her strength into the middle of the stream. De Forest and Sumpter both reached her at the same instant. Kate greeted them with a laugh of gratified roguery.

"I had never thought," said she, "to have two such gallant gentlemen in my train at the same time. I yield myself captive, and would thank each of you for

No. 10.

support, for verily I believe I never ran so fast in the whole course of my life."

"Miss Marvin," said Sumpter, "you have meddled with that it were better for woman——"

"Gallant Captain de Forest," interrupted Kate to that gentleman, who was retiring, "I certainly cannot dispense with your services—I thought you had too much courage to run both."

"Miss Marvin," rejoined De Forest, "with the assistance of the gentleman, whose aid you claim as a matter of course, my services can be dispensed with."

"Not so," responded Kate; "my breath is somewhat more free than it was at the end of my race; but after so gallant a chase, in your own nautical language, don't give up the ship. Besides, I have a few words for both of you."

De Forest waited, and with perfect nonchalance, she put her arm within his.

"There," she continued, "with a gallant and noble gentleman on each side, I may speak freely. Gentlemen, I know for what object you met this afternoon. Your principles and mine differ upon that subject, but do not fear a lecture from me—I am more disposed to laugh than moralise. But I have followed you on purpose to defeat the object of your meeting—I have accomplished my object for the present, and now let there be amity."

"Your feelings are those of a woman, Miss Marvin," rejoined De Forest; "your sex cannot rightly appreciate the calls of honour upon a brave man."

"No; happily for our sex, we are free from the obligations of truth and justice, and therefore released from the necessity of trying to shoot somebody at the mere calls of honour."

"Miss Marvin," said Sumpter—both gentlemen particularly designating her name, to prevent the supposition, on the part of either, that the remarks were general —"a gentleman of the cavalier school cannot appreciate the humility which teaches us, that if we receive a blow upon one cheek, we should turn the other also."

"I hardly thought that you would have even alluded to the teachings of one, whose mission was to women only, I suppose; as every precept inculcated by Him is at strange variance with the principles of what most honourable men call honour," rejoined Kate. "But I repeat, I have no disposition to lecture you; for those who dare do what they will acknowledge morally wrong, have an instinct of courage and honour, which I, at least, should never endeavour to convince by reason and argument."

The irony and emphasis of her remark were understood by both gentlemen, but they did not reply; as they reached the gathered members of their different parties,

"Gentlemen," said Kate, addressing the seconds, "I have spoiled your sport for to-day. And I have had my revenge upon these gentlemen, too," looking at Sumpter and De Forest, whose arms she retained, "for slighting my company. Miss Grant," she continued, "to your tender care I resign Mr. Sumpter, while I shall retain Captain de Forest as my prisoner."

Mr. Grant was too much displeased to make any remark; and supposing that Kate knew more of the matter than he did, he left it all to her care, unless a new turn of affairs required some decided action from him. The gentlemen who acted as seconds saw that the arrangements were taken out of their hands, for the time being at least, and remained silent spectators; for the presence of ladies was a new feature on "the field of honour."

De Forest, seriously displeased, knew not whether to treat Kate as he would a man under similar circumstances, or to be guided by the gallantry that rendered a lady's wishes almost imperious.

Lizzy was terrified. The actual state of the affair began to be apparent to her perceptions; and Sumpter's emotions, at this stage, were too compounded to admit of analyzation. For a few seconds there was silence, which De Forest interrupted by saying, as he endeavoured to release his arm, "Miss Marvin, I must be excused."

"The repetition of that phrase is unnecessary. You cannot be excused; nor shall I leave you unless you can run the fastest, and I believe I have shown you that even your heels in this case would be a useless expedient."

"I should suppose, madam, that your anxiety would be for your betrothed, and that he would share your vigilant care," rejoined De Forest.

"My betrothed!" responded Kate. "I know that this day I have been wooed after the eastern manner, where the swain gives chase to his lady-love, and is rewarded, by catching her. But I had two in my train, and one of them has already comforted himself with another damsel, while the other is constantly croaking, 'Wilt thou have me excused?'"

"Miss Marvin is surely aware of the common report, that Mr. Sumpter is engaged to the New-York belle," returned De Forest.

"The report, I believe, is correct; and if you will give me leave, I will have the pleasure of introducing you to her ladyship. Miss Grant," she continued, speaking in an undertone, "allow me to introduce to your good graces, the gallant Captain de Forest, of the United States Navy, but hereafter to be better known as one of the racers on Burton plantation meadow." The salutations exchanged were as cold and formal as might be.

"Mr. Grant," continued Kate, as her eye wandered over the meadow in search of something still missing, "permit me to extend to you also the introduction of Captain De Forest—a gentleman who is associated with many grateful and pleasant recollections, but whom, I never saw in such a churlish humour as I find him to-day."

"I was not aware," returned Mr. Grant, "that Captain de Forest had the pleasure of being your friend."

Kate's cheek reddened, and De Forest bit his lips.

"Sumpter," said Kate, " De Forest has already refused to introduce the gentleman whom I find in your company ; shall I ask you in vain ?"

"Certainly not," he replied; and immediately named the gentlemen.

The gentlemen bowed, and one of them remarked that "the present was the only place that he should not have been happy to meet Miss Marvin."

"All of you, gentlemen, to-day," returned Kate, "seem strangely forgetful of the deference which our sex expect under all circumstances. But I see we are likely to have an addition to our company." And directed by her own gaze, they turned and saw another lady and gentleman approaching them. The gentleman was advanced in years, and the lady somewhat his junior in age. From expecta tions as well as memory, Kate easily recognised the Mountain Woman ; but her companion was a stranger.

"You have done well," said the Mountain Woman, as her restless eye glanced around the group, and rested on Kate.

The old gentleman, who accompanied her, approached Sumpter.

"You have asked of me a mother and a brother," said he, addressing him ; "the one I give you in this lady, and the other in Legrand de Forest. And I should have supposed the event, which was to reveal them to you, had been too recent for me to have found you an actor in a scene like this."

"My mother!" said Sumpter, not heeding the closing reproof, "will you acknowledge me for a son ?"

She trembled with emotion, as she frantically clasped him to her breast without reply.

Amazement and sympathy were strangely blended in the countenances of those who witnessed the scene. To De Forest it was as unintelligible as to the others, and he stood as rigid as a statue.

"And will not a long-lost, but never forgotten brother, acknowledge me too ?" asked Sumpter, in a voice choked with emotion, holding out his hand, as his mother released him from her embrace.

De Forest grasped it. "It was not a dream then," said he, "that I had a brother—a father——"

"Who is no more," interrupted the old gentleman who had accompanied his mother.

The group around them instinctively retired a few paces, to allow the unmolested indulgence of their emotions. There is something sublime in the holy voice of nature and affection. They, who a moment before had proudly regarded each other as foes, now were closely locked in the embrace of fraternal regard. And were the veil of our own confined faculties and selfishness removed, perhaps we should recognise even in those we deem enemies, but the brothers of our own soul. Man, with his comprehension limited by circumstances and his own prejudices, regards his brother man with distrust and aversion—when, could the motives and the hearts of both be laid bare, they would leap to the embrace of kindness and love.

After their emotions were somewhat tranquillised, Sumpter, with a melancholy smile, and a voice trembling with the depth of his feelings, holding his mother and brother by the hand, advanced towards their friends.

"To a brother," said he, "I may offer an explanation, which I hesitated to give the man." And he briefly stated the circumstances of their misunderstanding.

When they were passing into the house in the morning, a crowd was gathered on the steps, all eagerly rushing the same way, as the expected speech of a prominent member had created great excitement. Sumpter was abstracted in his own thoughts upon the question that was coming up, and in his eagerness to get forward rudely jostled De Forest. De Forest, sensitive and irritated by his own reflections, thought that it bore the appearance of intentional rudeness, and demanded if such were intended.

"Perhaps so," replied Sumpter, neither heeding the question, nor him who asked it.

Quicker than thought, De Forest's sword was laid upon his shoulder. "If you are a man," said he, "you will not fear to answer for your unprovoked insult."

Those present immediately interfered, and the gentlemen were separated. But the wounded honour of De Forest could not be appeased by compulsion, and a challenge was conveyed and accepted. Sumpter would have considered himself disgraced to have offered an explanation, until after he had received his adversary's fire, which he intended not to return.

"And now," said he, after finishing his explanation, "in the presence of all here, I renounce firmly and deliberately, all obligations to the cavalier's code of honour. The provocation of an honourable man cannot require such deadly redress; and to those who cannot claim any title to be gentlemen, save their strength of nerve and dexterity in the use of sword or pistol, I do not hold myself answerable."

"Sumpter," said Mr. Grant, as a gleam of satisfaction crossed his features, "you have proved your true courage, by daring to renounce the prejudices of your education, in the presence of those who still deem them obligatory."

The approach of Kate's carriage interrupted him, and they all returned to the city.

Before they parted with the gentlemen who had come on to the ground as seconds, but who had truly been thirds, both brothers requested that, for the present at least, the developments of that day might remained confined to those present.

"Family reminiscences should never be made a matter of idle gossip, and our history remains for many mutual explanations," remarked Sumpter.

As they were entering their carriages, Mrs. Sumpter, whom we now recognise by her rightful name, took hold of Kate's hand,—

"Come," said she, "I would have all my new-found nestlings with me."

"The place does not belong to me," replied Kate. "But here is one," she added, pushing Lizzy forward, "who may claim the right." And beckoning to the old gentleman who had come with Mrs. Sumpter, she begged him to accept a seat with her and Mr. Grant, and ordered the driver onward.

"Well, I have been left,"—said Lizzy.

"Where you should be," interrupted Sumpter. "My mother and brother will also receive a daughter and a sister with me," he added, as he assisted her into the carriage.

CHAPTER XXV.

WHEN Mrs. Sumpter had been driven from her husband's house, as before detailed, she stood alone in the wide world. She had had no kindred—no friends save her husband's; but from them she shrank with dread. Conscious of no fault, unable to form even the most distant conjecture of what could have been the cause of her husband's conduct, her heart retreated within itself; and her only object was to escape from the hateful sight of mankind. Little Legrand was the only tie which bound her to life, and his helplessness was perhaps the only link in the chain which prevented an entire disseverment.

She remembered the executor of her aunt's legacy, and knowing him to be an honest man, sought his counsel and advice.

"I should advice you all means to return to your husband," said he, in answer to her interrogatory.

"Sir," she observed, "I am very much surprised that you should have given me such advice. Nothing is further from my thoughts than that. Notwithstanding the great reliance I place upon your discrimination and judgment, I must positively decline to follow your direction in the present instance."

"Of course you understand the peculiar position in which you are placed much better than I can; it would be advisable for you to act according to your own will."

"Exactly," replied Mrs. Sumpter.

A short pause now ensued.

"But there is another subject on which I should wish to ask your advice," she continued.

"In anything that I can be of service to you, I shall be most happy to do so," he answered.

"I am aware of it, and therefore apply to you for that counsel which I can obtain from no one else. My husband has had no provocation to the step he has been led to take—but let him do as he pleases, I'll never reproach him for it, nor will I now make any attempt to ascertain the cause, and I cannot profess contrition for a wrong which I am unconscious I have done."

A tear trembled on her eyelid at the painful thought this retrospection brought to her mind.

The worthy executor was grieved to see her thus affected and after a few moments had elapsed, he said,—

"Don't let the remembrance of any unpleasant subject depress your spirits, my dear madam."

"I will not."

The lady now looked more composed.

"What is the nature of the second subject on which you desire my advice," asked the executor.

"The investment of my money."

"Is it a large amount."

"No."

"How much?"

" About nine hundred pounds."

" What do you propose to invest it in?"

" Government securities," she replied.

" In that way it will yield a very small interest."

" But it will be safe."

" Certainly."

" Will it yield enough for me to live upon?"

" Scarcely," replied the executor.

" What can I do then?" she inquired.

" There are more profitable investments than the funds."

" What are they?"

" The canals."

" What interest should I obtain by investing my money in them?"

" Nearly ten per cent."

" Shall I invest in them?"

" I should advise you to do so."

" Will you see to the investment for me?"

" Willingly."

" Thank you."

While Mrs. Sumpter was writing out the necessary authorisation, the executor sat musing in his chair for a few moments, when these thoughts passed through his mind.

" What a strange world is this! Here are some seven or eight hundred millions of human beings, endowed in different degrees with those powers of discrimination and choice, which mark their superiority over the tribes of animate life by which they are surrounded; all busily striving to acquire a superiority of mind, wealth or condition, over their immediate fellows; and thus comes all of improvement—all of greatness, and much of misery which we see among men. Fortune's favours may be fickle and transitory—may change from side to side with inconstant vibration, but yet no more than the winds and the waves, does she control the whole destiny of man. Poets have sung—philosophers have taught, and fatalists nave proclaimed in all ages of the world, the potency of the frowns and the smiles of fortune; and with strange inconsistency, at the same time inculcating the idea that she is inconstant and changing, regardless of merit, and dispensing her favours in blindness, alike to the present and future. When one takes but a superficial view of society—glancing but along the surface, it appears indeed to be so. Or else, why does this man rise to wealth and eminence, and that other sink into poverty and obscurity, and to-morrow, by a freak of fortune, change their relative conditions in life? The wretched and miserable are the strongest believers in the caprice of fortune; the wealthy and prosperous are willing to dispense with her aid, as more satisfaction can be drawn from the belief that their success is the consequence of their own sagacity and foresight. In a pecuniary point—where the acquisition and loss of wealth are taken into the account, fortune operates strangely oftentimes."

She now rose to depart.

" Before you go, is there anything else in which I can serve you?"

" I desire nothing more, thank you;" and wishing the executor good morning, she departed, the executor having promised to invest the money, and to come to her shortly to communicate the result.

She shortly afterwards retired to as unbroken seclusion as a city residence could be made. Years passed in monotony. To the child she denied nothing that his fancy desired, or his good required. To herself she allowed no indulgence.

As Legrand grew older, he became more inquisitive; and to give his thoughts a new turn, and herself the benefit of air and exercise, she removed into the country as related in the commencement of our tale.

Her own imaginative temperament, with her peculiar sorrows, combined to unsettle her reason, and she fancied vague dreams, that her isolation was a decree of Providence, to keep her from the idolatry of loving earthly objects. Guided by this supposition, her manner towards Legrand was so cold and fixed, that he learned to doubt whether she was indeed his mother.

After he left her, she remained in her mountain house, until the inquiries of her husband and son alarmed her, and she departed for another residence unknown even to Legrand. That she resided where she knew of his movements, was evident, as she always met him, whether he was at New York, Philadelphia, Baltimore, or Washington.

A few weeks before the events of the last chapter, she had joined him at Washington, intending to reveal herself to her eldest son, as she knew her husband was dead. She had only waited for the presence and testimony of the gentleman who was the only repository of her secret, but who, from age and infirmity had been unable to grant her request, until a few days previously. He had not then arrived in the city, but awaited her summons at a friend's, a few miles distant.

When Legrand returned, after his encounter with Sumpter, she instantly noted the turmoil of his mind ; and although she religiously denied herself the luxury of expressed anxiety, yet her watchfulness and care was almost superhuman. At four o'clock in the afternoon, she was in possession of all the details of the expected meeting.

Her alarm gifted her with more sanity and directness of purpose than she was wont to use, and she instantly saw the necessity of a development of the mystery which her own life had woven. Fearing that her assertion alone might be regarded as anxiety for Legrand's safety, rather than fact, she wrote the note to Kate, trusting that the fertility of her imagination could prevent the meeting by some expedient, until she could produce the testimony necessary to support the truth of their relationship. The results of her measures have been heretofore detailed.

The reunion of relatives so long severed, was as happy and mutually pleasing, as the ardent desire of both of the young men for justice, love and kindness, could make it. Both strove to win their mother from the dreamy halo of imagination, to the truth of reality.

As Legrand chose not to assume his father's name unless he left the navy, their history was confined to the few to whom accident or connection had rendered it necessary to be revealed.

A short time after the events of the fortunately bloodless duel, Kate accompanied the marquis and Donna Maria to a splendid party, given by another of the foreign ministers.

During the evening, as she was engaged in an animated conversation with a distinguished gentleman present, whose brow was encircled with the laurels of both a warrior and a statesman, and who since then, both by his life and his death, has written his name in enduring characters upon the page of his country's history, her attention was drawn to the entrance of De Forest, by the gentleman with whom she was conversing.

" And there comes Captain de Forest, of whom I can say, that not a braver or more gallant gentleman claims the honour of being an American. Miss Marvin, I must introduce you to the gentleman ;" and he beckoned him to approach.

Neither betrayed their previous acquaintance, and passed the salutations of the introduction as strangers.

" And now, Miss Marvin," continued the gallant general, " it is but justice for me to inform you that Captain De Forest regards beauty as an enemy, and never surrendered to its attacks—and I shall leave it to your discretion whether to attempt his heart by siege or storm."

" But, general," replied Kate, " you have assured me that he never surrenders. Surely you would not have me throw away my time and forces upon an impregnable fortress. Besides," she added, with a slight degree of constraint, " I am already aware of Captain De Forest's impregnability, having held him a long time under close siege, and more recently attacked him by storm. There was not the slightest intention of capitulation evinced in either case."

" Although I dislike to dispute a lady's veracity," rejoined De Forest, " truth compels me to correct Miss Marvin's statement of facts. In the case of the siege the stronghold of the fortress was entirely subdued, and when I asked the opportunity of honourable capitulation, it was denied. The object of storm was a matter of doubt, and I was disposed to consider it the defence of a more valued object."

"Excuse me," said the general, who instantly perceived the true bearing of the matter, "I would speak with Mr. Clayton, whom I see approaching—and I am sure I could not resign Miss Marvin to more desirable company."

"The heat of the room is oppressive," remarked De Forest; "allow me to conduct you to a cooler seat?"

She assented, by taking his proffered arm; and in another room, within the retired recess of a window, he paused and said,—

"This is indeed a happy moment for me."

"I thought, perhaps, you would not have been here to-night," said Kate.

"How could you think so?" exclaimed De Forest, with much fervour, "how could you think I would not come, when I knew you were here?"

"You men are so feeble, so wayward. I thought, perhaps, you would not come if it were only because I wanted to speak to you."

"How could you be so unjust—how could you judge me so unkindly?" asked De Forest, apparently with much feeling. "If you knew me better—if you could only read my heart!"

"I'm sure I wish I could," said Kate.

"I wish you could indeed," replied De Forest; "you would think better of me. You would not find me the cold, trifling creature which I fear you now think me. Ah! I wish you could see into my heart, you would think well of me. You would read much that I dare not utter. You think I am unfeeling, because I do not express my feelings—because I am miserably—most miserably tongue-tied."

His voice faltered, and his head drooped.

"And why tongue-tied?" asked Kate.

"You need not ask—you know but too well," replied De Forest, in a melancholy tone; "there is much which I might have said—much that I should have said long ago—much which I have long wanted to say; but how can I? My heart may be full to bursting, and yet I must be silent. I have no right to speak to you on any other than common topics; but do not therefore think that I am trifling. Judge me not by what I say, but by what I feel; and believe that I do feel much more than I dare utter."

"I will believe it," said Kate.

"Spoken like yourself, kind, generous girl," he said, looking up into her face with a countenance beaming with admiration and love. "I shall be happier now, oh, much happier—not happy," he continued, more sorrowfully, "that I can never be—but happier now that you no longer think me cold and heartless."

"Why not happy," asked Kate with much eagerness; "you can, you will be very happy."

"Never."

"Why not?"

"Don't ask me—do not ask me," returned De Forest, in despairing accents; "I cannot put the answer into words; but you may read it in my face—you may hear it in my faltering voice. It has been my own fault. I ought to have known better."

"Better than what?"

"Better than to have sought your friendship—better than to have believed that I could see you often—could often converse with you—could often enjoy your society and friendship—and not—not pay the penalty of my rashness. I had almost said what it would be wrong for you to hear without chiding me."

"What is that?"

"I dare not tell."

"But I will know," said Kate.

"It is, then, my deep—my fervent love."

What followed it is impossible for me to say. I can only state that the only time Kate Marvin was ever speechless, was when she would have said "yes," to some question asked by De Forest. She turned her eyes, humid with delight and emotion, upon his beaming face, and—and—

But we do not care to say what that look promised, or what De Forest gave in return for it. What matter if the rooms were thronged with company? Dear reader, if you are a gallant gentleman, I am sure you would yield to the same temptation, were a pair of beautiful eyes telling you of love and confidence, and sweet and pouting lips as ever were woman's, close to your own.

And if my reader is a lady, I am sure she would not feel disposed to resent a like liberty, under like circumstances.

Sumpter and Lizzy, who were promenading the rooms, approached the same window. They were about to retire, but seeing who occupied it, joined them. The heightened colour of Kate's cheek, and the manly, gratified emotion of De Forest, neere tell-tales.

"I should think," said Lizzy archly, to Kate, "that you and De Forest had been on a blackberry expedition."

No. 11

A short time after Lizzy and Kate had parted for the night, Doctor Sprague approached her, to whom she said.——

"What a very tedious, long day it has been, doctor!" as she languidly seated herself on the sofa, and drew her beautiful white hand over her face, to conceal a yawn she could not overcome.

"You are fatigued with your exertions, I presume," said her friend, looking compassionately upon her. "Permit me to inquire what have been your employments during this long, tedious day."

"Employments?" repeated the young lady, colouring. "Oh, for that matter, I cannot remember all I have done."

"But you can enumerate some things, no doubt. Have you walked, or rode, or read, or worked?"

"I detest walking when the wind is so high, and the streets so dusty. Why, no lady of fashion would be seen abroad to-day," replied Lizzy, with great vivacity.

"And so, of course, I may conclude you have neither walked nor rode," observed Doctor Sprague, as he very composedly put on his spectacles, and surveyed the countenance of Lizzy through them, with an air as deliberate as a fop levels his eye-glass at the theatre. Lizzy, however, shrunk more from the doctor's scrutiny than she would have done from the fop's. "Well, reading and working may be performed when the wind is high and the streets dusty."

Lizzy was silent, for reading came next in course, and she was too well acquainted with the doctor to attempt to impose on him by pretending to have read books, which she knew only by their titles or the reviews. Some young ladies may think Lizzy very conscientious. They see no harm in palming off a little of that smattering of knowledge, which they gain by mingling in society, as their own. Why could not Lizzy have named some book which the old gentleman never heard of, and then, if she did mistake names, and misapply characters, misquote sentiment, he would never have detected her. Many a young lady has thus rattled away, to her own great delight and fancied importance, when with those who she deemed could not readily discover if she was ignorant whether the authors she so familiarly named, wrote in prose or poetry, or whether the book she pretended so lately to have read, was a sermon or a song.

"Have you read Heber's Travels yet?" resumed the doctor, attempting by a question, to oblige her to converse.

"No—not at all—not much," returned Lizzy, speaking very quick. "I am not interested in it, doctor. I always hated a diary. It looks so methodistic and mechanical. I think no author can be so particular, without having, in all his actions and speeches, reference to the note-book. Can thoughts be free, when one is subjected to the trammel of entering them all on the diary, as regularly a a merchant would his accounts? I would not, for the universe, undertake to be thus particular; and I always pity the writers of such minute facts too much to enjoy the information their labours would otherwise afford me."

"But there is one care which oppresses you, which the good bishop seldom if ever appears to have felt. He never had to endure a very tedious, long day," said the doctor, smiling.

"Will keeping a dairy always preserve us from ennui?" demanded Lizzy.

"The endeavour to have something worthy to record, would preserve us, my dear. The industrious and the studious seldom complain of a very tedious, long day."

"Now, I shall hear that saying of mine for this whole season, I presume," replied the laughing girl, as she took her friend's hand, and affectionately pressed it between both hers. "Yet I said it merely because I did not at the time think of any observation more wise. I forgot how very circumspect it was necessary to be——"

"When conversing with your old fashioned friend," interrupted the doctor.
"Well, well, I forgive you. But, in this age of energy and improvement, nothing strikes me more unpleasantly, except gross vice, than to see young people idle, and

hear their listless complaints of the tediousness of time. 1 can very well believe that the days must be tedious and long tc those of your sex, excluded as you are from the business and bus'le of the world, who have no literary resources. But now, when we men are willing, not only to allow you have talents, but even to encourage you to employ them, the woman who wastes her time in frivolous pursuits or fashionable amusements—and such people are those who oftenest complain of very tedious, long days—deserves to be despised.

"But you don't mean to say, do you, that I waste my time?" she inquired. "You would not if you knew all," she continued, archly.

"All what?"

"You'll know in a short time."

"But I want to know now."

"You must have patience."

"1 have but a small stock of it."

"I know it," she replied, laughing, "and am determined to make you put it to the utmost tension."

"That's too bad."

"Not at all."

The doctor looked vexed at her inflexibility.

"I'll be bound to say that there's nothing more happened than what I already suspect," he said, thinking to draw the information out of her by pretending to know what she determined to keep secret.

"I'll be bound you don't know.

"But I do."

"Well, what is it?"

"I shan't tell."

"Because you don't know."

"Oh, yes, I do."

"Then out with it at once ; and we shall see if they are the same.

"You'll tell me afterwards what it is, if I should happen to be wrong in my conjecture?"

"I will if you, say at once what you guess has taken place."

"Well, then, I suppose 1 must. It appears to me that you and Kate have been putting your heads together as to the best means of playing off some of your jokes upon me the next time we meet."

"Is that what you thought?"

"Yes."

"I assure you that nothing of the kind has been proposed."

"Indeed."

"It's true."

"I must believe it, as you tell me so."

The doctor could scarcely repress a smile at the manner in which he had induced Lizzy to tell him what he was so desirous to know.

"Well, to show how deceived you were, I have to tell you that Kate is at last to be married."

"Well, who's the lucky fellow?"

"Captain de Forest."

"And is there no other wedding you have to tell me about?"

Lizzy blushed.

"Ah, I thought so," continued the doctor.

Still Lizzy made no answer.

"I say that you must have patience. I merely promised to tell you about Kate, and therefore you must be satisfied."

Having said this, she arose and hastily left him.

The next morning Kate and Lizzy were alone, and the latter was arranging that Kate's nuptials should be celebrated at the same time with her own. "I do not now about that," rejoined Kate.

"About what?" asked De Forest, who had entered without ceremony with Sumpter.

"That I shall wholly forgive a certain Captain de Forest, for the very marked neglect which he exhibited towards me some two months ago, after he was informed that I was in Washington, by the gentleman with whose family I was remaining."

"But you know, dearest, that I thought my brother was the happy man—and I could not see you, and think that another was to possess the object that had been woven in every dream of my life."

The two weddings were arranged to take place at the close of the session of Congress. We are not in possession of the particulars—but we may safely presume that the ceremonial was associated with the consciousness of present happiness, and glowing hope of the future; the realization of the highest expectations of both Kate and Lizzy, and their brother husbande.

* * * * * * *

We have little to add in conclusion—nevertheless, custom desires that some disposition should be made of a few of the most prominent characters introduced in the course of our narrative.

Mrs. Sumpter accompanied her eldest son to her early home, and after a few years of sorrowful retrospection, was laid by her husband's side.

The marquis and Donna Maria, who felt a continuous interest in Kate, rejoiced in her union to one to whom they were all so much indebted in the strife at sea. Their correspondence with her, after their return to their native land, contained many postscripts by Carlos, whose gratitude to his fair deliverer was equalled only by his admiration of her excellent qualities of mind and heart.

Mr. and Mrs. Lee may be said merely to exist. She and her children enjoy the blessings of a home in her father's house; and the Washingtonians have some slight hopes of redeeming her husband from the degradation of vices to which he has long been addicted.

Mr. Thompson returned to the west shortly after the union of Kate and Lizzy to their respective partners and married the Kentucky lady, to whom he referred in his stump speech on the rural occasion. He has won his way to wealth and renown.

Dan Grant and his "wee wife" pursue the even tenour of their way, afar from the dusty paths of a jostling world. Mary is a loving and domestic spouse; and Dan has settled down to books and the plough.

Aunt Martha still lives, to enjoy the happiness of the affectionate regard of her kindred and friends. She also still occasionally tries her wit, as usual, upon Doctor Sprague. That worthy philosopher retains all his old opinions, and has discovered some "new things under the sun." The latest of his remarks of which we have heard, related to the cause of Mrs. Strong's death. In his judgment, that lady died of friction of the tongue.

THE END.